CLEAN FAST-PACED ACTION THRILLERS

JOIN THE READER'S LIST

Get the latest releases and exclusive giveaways - sign up to the Alex Cage Reader List:

www.AlexCage.com/signup

ALSO BY ALEX CAGE

Orlando Black Series

Carolina Dance

Bayside Boom

Family Famous (Novella)

Bet on Black

Leroy Silver Series

Contracts & Bullets

Aloha & Bullets

Get the latest releases and exclusive giveaways, sign up to the Alex Cage Reader List.

www.AlexCage.com/signup

BET ON BLACK

AN ORLANDO BLACK NOVEL

ALEX CAGE

BET ON BLACK

CHAPTER
ONE

THERE I STOOD, in the corner of a square ring, under the
night sky, in the middle of a valley, and in the middle of
another fine mess. A crowd of nearly a hundred surrounded
the ring. All yelling and cheering. In the opposite corner
stood a muscular man wearing a mohawk and red shorts.
Wearing MMA gloves, he pounded his hairy chest before gritting his teeth and narrowing his sights on me. Another man,
wearing dark pants and a white shirt, stood at the center of
the ring.

The man in the white shirt pointed at me. "Ready, black?"
he said. Not because of my name or my skin complexion, but
because I wore black trousers and a black tank top.

I nodded.

He then pointed to the guy in the shorts. "Ready, red?"

The hairy-chested man nodded.

"Fight!" the guy at the center of the ring shouted before
stepping back.

A bell dinged, and I walked toward the ring's center while
the guy in the red shorts raced toward me with his fist drawn
back. He swung at my jaw. I bobbed under the punch, then
quickly pivoted to face his back with my hands at guard. My

opponent spun toward me while hurling a back fist at my head. I ducked beneath the attack and shuffled backward. The crowd's cheers grew louder.

The man's nostrils flared and his teeth gritted as he charged. He threw a kick, but I parried it. As I back-stepped, my attacker shuffled toward me and continued his assault with the combination I was waiting on. He jabbed at me with his left. I parried it. Then his right. I slipped inside the punch, and just as I expected, the man hesitated. In that split second of hesitation, I raised my left arm and exposed my ribcage. My opponent took the bait and launched a kick. Before he could connect, I darted to him and delivered a hard elbow to the side of his face. The man stumbled back and doubled over. I closed the gap between us and kneed his face. As he groaned and flopped backward, I skipped-step toward him and planted my heel into his solar plexus. He landed on the ropes, then flipped over and out of the ring. I followed the referee to the ring's edge and saw my opponent sprawled on the floor.

The referee ducked between the ropes, then knelt and lifted the man's head from the ground before saying something to him and moving the fingers of his free hand in the fighter's face. After a few seconds, the ref stood, crossed his arms, then slung them apart. The bell dinged, and the referee crawled back into the ring and raised my arm. Cheers and applause came from the crowd as I snatched my arm away from the ref and turned toward my corner. The person I was looking for wasn't there, so I scanned the other three corners, but still couldn't find him.

As I hopped from the ring, two men hoisted the guy in the red shorts to his feet. I walked past and threaded through the crowd with my head on a swivel, searching for the missing DEA agent. The pats on my back and shouts from the crowd followed me all the way to a passageway for the locker room. I walked through the passage alone and to a dirt field illuminated by large construction flood lights. A pair of mobile homes flanked me on either side. A third home sat on the far end with a flagpole out front. That was where the lockers were. As I made my way across the field toward it, a guard armed with an MP5 approached me.

"Good fight, Ghost," he said with a smile. "You're so quick, the fight didn't even last that long. I bet on you, so I made some money tonight."

"That's great," I said. "The guy I was with earlier, have you seen 'em?"

The guard pursed his lips and shook his head. "Not since he was with you."

"Alright. Thanks," I said before continuing toward the portable home.

"See you around, champ," the guard said to my back.

The portable home was empty inside. I hustled to the locker room, opened my locker, then changed into my jeans and t-shirt. Before slipping into my boots, I made sure my dual knife holsters were secure around my ankles. Once fully dressed, I checked my phone, but found no missed calls or messages. I exited the portable and walked back to the ring area, where the crowd roared in encouragement for an ongoing match. Weaving through the mob, I kept an eye out for my missing DEA agent, but there was still no sign of him. I continued through the crowd, then into a passageway which led out of the valley.

As I exited the passageway, two men in black suits armed with MP5s stood on either side of the entrance. One of them nodded at me as I dodged a line of people and walked onto an enormous field full of parked cars. And not just any cars. Bentleys, Ferraris, and Lamborghinis were all present, but the car I was looking for wasn't as extravagant. It was a dented, silver Ford Focus in need of new tires and a new paint job. When I located the car, I peeked through the window hoping to find the DEA agent who also happened to be my chauffeur but was disappointed when he wasn't there and wondered how I'd get back to my motel room since he had the car's key.

At that thought, I heard a fuss coming from the passageway entrance. When I glanced over my shoulder, I saw the missing agent exiting, but he wasn't alone. Two men trailed behind him. Both were fit, both had ivory skin, both wore a suit with no tie, but one had spiky blond hair while the other had short brown hair. A short man with a gray suit and a ponytail followed close behind them, carrying a brief-case. While keeping my eyes on the group of men, I ducked and circled the Ford's trunk to the passenger side. They all entered a black Porsche Cayenne before cruising out of the parking area and up the dirt road. I removed a knife from my ankle holster, then raced to the front driver's side door of the Focus. With my face turned from the door, I smashed the butt of the knife into the window. The glass shattered, and I used my knife to rake away the loose shards before reaching my arm through and unlocking the door. Using the knife, I poked the steering column and pried it open, then spend the next few minutes relearning how to hot wire a car. When I connected the correct wires, the Focus revved to life. I swept the glass from the seat and slid in behind the wheel. I backed from the parking area, flicked on the headlights, then sped down the road. The road was dim and the Cayenne was nowhere in sight. Not a glint from a taillight, not even a silhouette of the vehicle, just darkness.

Lost them. Not good.

After a minute of driving, I approached two SUVs parked perpendicular on either side of the road. Neither one was the Cayenne. At each SUV, there was the shadow of a man holding a gun. I slowed down and one of them recognized me and nodded. After returning the nod, I rode past. I monitored them in my rear-view mirror until they completely disap-peared into the darkness of the night. The Focus droned up the rough, dirt road for another twenty minutes before smooth pavement caressed its tires. I removed my phone, flipped it open, pressed at it, and held it to my ear. It rang and rang, but no one answered.

"Another missing agent," I muttered to myself. "Not good."

I drove another hour before trying the number again. And like before, no answer.

Where are you?

After stopping for gas and driving another forty minutes, I arrived at my motel, but I didn't pull into the parking lot because something caught my attention. The Porsche Cayenne sat parked a few spaces from my room. I made a note of the license plate number, then continued a quarter of a mile up the road before turning into a local diner's parking lot. Inside the diner, the smell of burgers and fries and customer chit chat filled the space, and as I made my way to the counter eyes from unknown faces followed me. I grabbed a napkin and a to-go menu off the countertop before hearing a voice.

"Hi," the voice said.

I turned to see a slim woman with silky dirty-blonde hair approaching me.

She smiled. "Gonna have dinner with us, Mr. White?"

It took me a split second to process everything before saying, "I sure am, but I'm going to take it to go."

"Ahh, you're not staying here with me tonight?"

"Nope. I'm sorry," I said with a smile.

She smiled again. "So, what are you having?"

"I'll have what I had last night."

"Grilled chicken, brown rice, and steamed broccoli, right?"

"You remembered," I said with my eyebrows raised.

"Of course. Most people around here don't eat like that. I'll get this in for you," she said as she pivoted away from me.

"Thanks—hey."

The waitress turned to face me.

"Do you have a pen?" I asked.

"Sure. Plenty of 'em," she said while handing me a pen from her apron pocket.

"Thanks."

She smiled, then made her way toward the kitchen.

On the napkin I wrote, *After the fight, Vargas left with Long, Snyder, and a short man with a ponytail. Black Porsche Cayenne LPN MXC-F144*, then finished with, *It's parked in front of my motel room*. At the top, I wrote the date and time, then used the menu to create an envelope before placing the napkin inside and folding it shut. I exited the diner, crossed the street, and walked twenty yards in the motel's direction before reaching a slightly worn mail drop box. I placed the folded menu inside, then made my way back to the diner where I sat at the counter for five minutes before the waitress brought me my food.

"Here you go," she said while placing my bag and ticket on the table.

The bill was eighteen dollars. I gave her thirty.

"That's all yours," I said.

"Thanks. Will I see you for dinner tomorrow?"

"Possibly. And maybe the next few days after."

"Well, I'll be here tomorrow night, but the next few nights after, I'll be working late at the mall. There's a large shipment coming in, and we're rearranging the store. Just in case you come and I'm not here."

"I'll keep that in mind," I said on my way to the door.

"See you around, Anthony."

I entered the Focus and placed my food on the passenger seat and removed my flip phone. I tried the number I called earlier and again got no answer.

Something's off.

I backed the car out and veered onto the road toward the motel. The Cayenne was no longer there. I parked, grabbed my food, then walked to my motel room. Before opening the door, I placed my ear to it and listened, but heard nothing. Multiple scenarios played in my mind. They could've really left, or were lurking around waiting to ambush me, but for what? I was sure they didn't want to physically harm me, so I unlocked my door and opened it. And when I saw inside, suddenly I wasn't so sure anymore.

CHAPTER
TWO

TRUTH BE TOLD, I wasn't completely sure about anything since two days prior, when it all started. I was driving through a small town five miles west of San Antonio, Texas. It was a sunny and comfortable afternoon, and I had just finished gassing up my black Dodge Viper GTS when I heard a faint grunt. I walked to the opposite side of the empty gas station and saw a group of men tussling in the dirt near the back of the station. My gut told me to go back to my car and leave, because given my history, my good deeds usually cost me a day or even a week of headache. Going against my better judgment, I walked across the pavement and onto the dry grainy dirt where three men stood in front of me. Two on one side, and one on the other, all with their fists raised. The two standing together looked similar. Both wore jeans and a t-shirt. Both had toned physiques and ivory freckled skin, but one had spiky blond hair while the other had short brown hair. The guy opposite them wore dark blue jeans and a dirty white polo shirt. His hair was dark and messy, and his beard and mustache were bushy on his almond-colored face. The man with the short brown hair feinted a jab at the man across from him. Keeping his fist raised, the guy in the polo shirt shuffled back with his eyes locked on the two men in front of him.

"Now two on one, that doesn't seem fair," I said to the group of men.

The guy with the blond hair glanced over his shoulder. "Mind your business and move along," he said.

At that moment, the brown-haired guy threw a cross and connected to the jaw of the man with the bushy beard. The man fell to the ground and a cloud of dust rose around him. He rolled to his side and crawled to a kneeling position.

"No, I think I'll stick around and see how this plays out," I said before walking toward the fallen man. Halfway there, I heard footsteps closing in behind me.

"I thought I said get lost," the blond guy's voice growled.

As I turned, his fist darted toward my face. I weaved outside of his punch and delivered a solid hook to the guy's ribcage. He dropped to the ground and wormed in the dirt as his partner with the low cut directed his attention at me.

"You'll pay for that," he said, knitting his eyebrows and gritting his teeth.

I shrugged and rolled my eyes.

The man pivoted on his right leg before kicking at me with a roundhouse. I stepped inside his attack, caught his kicking leg at my side, and hooked it with my arm before sweeping his other leg from under him. It happened in one quick, smooth motion. So quick, the guy didn't realize it happened until he descended to the ground. I saw the whites of his eyes grow larger and his mouth open wide as he plummeted. When his back smacked the ground, I heard a breath forced from his mouth. I shook my head at the sight of the two men squirming on the ground, then walked to the bushy bearded guy.

"How did you get on their bad side?" I asked, while grabbing his arm and helping him to his feet.

And to my surprise, the guy yanked his arm away, then shoved me.

"Whatcha do?" he said.

"Thought I was helping you."

"I never asked for help, amigo."

"So, you enjoy getting punched in the face?"

The man's gaze fell to the ground, then on the two men in the dirt, then back to me before finally across the highway, beyond a parked dark-blue sedan, and into the desert field.

After a few seconds, and no verbal response from him, I shrugged and walked back to my car. I got behind the wheel and watched as the bushy faced guy helped the other two men to their feet. The three walked further behind the gas station. The bushy bearded guy kept peering over his shoulder and across the highway at the dark-blue sedan.

When the men were out of sight, the sedan slowly pulled off. I found it strange, but an hour earlier I saw a woman casually walking around the outside of a Whataburger with an assault rifle, and no one batted an eye. And thirty minutes before that, I saw a man eat a cinnamon roll the size of his head, so three guys fist fighting wasn't too shocking or unbelievable. I started my car, veered onto the highway, and drove eight miles southeast until I reached a hotel. Figured I'd turn in for the day and continue heading east the next day. I checked in at the front desk, then went to my room, carrying only a change of jeans and a white t-shirt with me. A pine smell struck my nose as I entered. Light permeated through a large window and filled the spacious room. I tossed my clothes on the bed before patting the comforter. The linen was soft and wrinkle free, perfect for a good night's sleep. And I wouldn't find out until the next day just how much I'd need it.

· · ·

I rolled from the bed and onto the floor early the next morning. Inside the dim room, I performed two hundred push-ups, then one hundred sit-ups followed my thirty minutes of forms and shadow boxing before concluding with some tai chi movements and breathing exercises. The sun had risen above the horizon by the time I'd finished a steamy shower and shrugged into my clothes. I brushed the bushy hair on my head and face before concluding I should see a barber soon. My stomach growled and since I skipped dinner the night before, the next thing on my mind was breakfast.

Downstairs, the aroma from eggs, grits, sausage, biscuits, and coffee stuffed the area. It was the smell of the typical continental breakfast. I thanked the dining room staff and ate a bit of everything before washing it down with black coffee and heading to the front desk.

"Checking out," I said to a slender, dirty-blonde woman behind the desk while handing her my keycard.

"Thank you, sir. How was your stay?" she asked as she typed on a keyboard.

"Brief."

She smiled and typed for a few more seconds before looking at me and saying, "Okay, sir, you're all taken care of."

"Thank you," I told her before walking out of the hotel.

I went to my car and placed my dirty clothes in the trunk, and as I circled to the front of the Viper, I heard a voice.

"Hot ride," a woman said.

I glanced in the voice's direction and saw a woman approaching. She wore boots, jeans, and a brown biker jacket. Her skin was a silky espresso tone, slightly darker than mine, and her eyes hid behind a pair of shades.

"Thanks, she's a beauty," I said, while scanning the parking lot.

"That she is," the woman said. She then used her fingers to rake strands of her natural, shoulder-length, curly hair behind her ear.

As she walked to the Viper's hood and leaned against it, I caught a glimpse of her badge and gun. I glanced around the parking lot and spotted the same dark-blue sedan I saw the day before. It sat parked at the front of the hotel, near the east far corner.

I nodded in the sedan's direction. "You have a hot ride, too."

She followed my gaze, then placed her sights back on me before scoffing and smiling. "Yeah, I guess so," she said with a chuckle, still leaning on the hood.

"Well, we both have hot rides. I'll be on my way now."

"Not so fast, Mr. Orlando James Black," she said standing from the car.

"Oh, you used my full name. I must be in trouble."

"Maybe. That all depends on you," she said while waving the sedan over.

As the vehicle pulled from the parking space, she placed her hand near her hip, on the same side as her firearm.

"What are you carrying, Glock 19?"

"No, a seventeen, and I'm pretty good with it."

I chuckled. "I bet you are. Mind telling me what you're doing?"

"I will."

The sedan stopped beside us, and from the front passenger's side, a woman with caramel hair flowing down her back exited. She had tanned skin, and her height and clothing matched the other woman's except her biker jacket was black instead of brown.

"Aren't you required to tell me who you are?" I asked the woman with the natural, curly hair.

"Am I?"

"Yeah, usually law enforcement is. Dark sedan, Glock 17. I'm guessing you're not local law enforcement. What are you DEA, FBI?"

"Special Agent Deidra Harris, DEA," she said while flapping her jacket and exposing her badge.

I'd seen fake badges before, but hers wasn't one of them. It was legit.

"Okay, Agent Deidra Harris, what do you want with me?"

"We'll get to that," she said as the woman with the caramel-colored hair approached us. Deidra pointed at her. "This is Special Agent Jessica Ward."

Jessica's eyes slowly traced from my feet to my face. She then leaned toward Deidra. "He's handsome," she said.

Deidra scoffed a chuckle, and as she did, the sedan's front driver's side door opened. On the opposite side of the roof, the upper body of a stocky man with silver hair appeared. He circled the car to where the group of us stood.

"This is Special Agent William Anson," Deidra said introducing him.

Anson rubbed his hand across his silver, full beard and just stared at me.

"Okay, now what?" I asked with a shrug.

"We're going for a ride," Deidra said.

I glanced at my car, then back at her.

"Don't worry, Mr. Black," she said. "Your car will be fine."

"Are you charging me with something?" I asked.

"Not at the moment."

"Then I don't have to take a ride with you—"

"But I can charge you with obstruction," she said interrupting me.

"Obstruction?"

"Yep. So, either come quietly, or in cuffs. The choice is yours."

I stared at her for a moment before sighing and walking toward the sedan's back passenger side door.

"You can ride shotgun," she said while pointing to the front door. "I insist."

I shook my head before walking to the door, opening it, and sliding into the sedan. Deidra and Jessica entered the back while Anson sat behind the wheel.

Another fine mess, I thought, as Anson started the car and pulled out of the parking lot.

CHAPTER
THREE

TEN MINUTES LATER, we veered into the driveway of a gated, eight-story, off-white brick building in downtown San Antonio. Anson lowered his window as he stopped at the guard hut. A security guard stepped out, then waved Anson through as if he knew him. Anson drove inside and toward the parking garage, where he found a spot close to the entrance. We exited the car, entered the building, and walked past a security station in an empty lobby before taking the elevator to the fifth floor. The elevator dinged, the doors slid apart, and we stepped into a foyer where a pair of large glass double doors met us.

"I got it," Jessica said, while lifting a card from her pocket and waving it across a small square panel next to the double doors.

The doors clicked, and Jessica pulled open one side.

"C'mon in, Mr. Black," Deidra said as she walked through the doorway.

I followed her in while Jessica held the door open. Anson grabbed the door and nodded for Jessica to enter before him.

"Such a gentleman," she said.

Anson grunted.

I followed Deidra down a short hallway and onto an office floor. At the center were cubicle desks and computers and tables. Individuals walked up and down the floor and conversed with one another.

"This way, Mr. Black," Deidra said pointing to her right.

The four of us walked in that direction, passing more office furniture and agents on our way to a room. Inside was a rectangular table with two chairs across from one another.

"Have a seat, Mr. Black," Deidra said.

I stared at her for a moment before shaking my head and walking toward the chair facing the door. On my way, I noticed a double-sided mirror to my right.

"I'll be in my office if you girls need anything," Anson said before leaving the room.

"Make yourself comfortable, Mr. Black," Deidra said. "Do you want anything? Water or coffee?"

"I'll take a coffee," I said.

Deidra nodded at Jessica, who walked toward the door before turning and asking me, "How do you take your coffee? Cream and sugar?"

"Straight black, please."

Jessica smiled, then walked out of the room.

"I'll be back," Deidra said as she walked to the door herself.

"How long are you going to keep me here?" I asked.

"Shouldn't be too long, but that'll largely depend on you," she said before exiting the room.

As the door clunked shut, I sat and stared in its direction, drumming my fingers on the tabletop. Three minutes later, Jessica entered the room with a steaming, white Styrofoam cup in hand.

She placed the cup on the table. "Anything else I can get you?"

"Answers," I said.

"Deidra will fill you in," she said before smiling and walking out.

Fill me in? I thought, while sipping my coffee. I drank half the cup before the door opened and Deidra entered, carrying a manilla folder. She dropped the folder on the table as she sat in the chair across from me. I looked into her eyes. They showed strength and vulnerability.

"Okay, Mr. Black. Who are you, really?" she asked.

I shrugged. "You've been calling me Mr. Black all morning, so let's stick with that." I nodded toward the double mirror. "Do we have an audience?"

Deidra's eyebrows knitted. "Audience?" she said while looking at the mirror. "No, this'll be a private conversation. Just between you and I."

"What's in the folder?"

"You."

I squinted.

Deidra picked up the folder and opened it. "Let's see," she said, looking into the folder. "In the foster system at a very young age. Wow, they sure kept you in a lot of different martial art classes growing up." She read in silence for a moment. "Huh. Your senior year of high school was very interesting," she said while looking at me with a raised eyebrow.

I said nothing.

"Okay. So you went into the army, spent some time as a Ranger and a Delta Force member. Very impressive. Then there's a few years of redaction before you settled in Asia." Deidra closed the folder and dropped it on the table. "Who are you?" she asked.

I shrugged and nodded at the folder. "I guess I'm whatever's in there," I said.

Deidra crinkled her nose and shook her head. "Nah, that was then. Who are you now?"

"Are you charging me with something?"

Deidra hunched her shoulders and stood. "I don't want to," she said as she walked to the door.

I watched as she opened it and waved to someone on the outside.

"But I can," she continued, walking back to the table.

Seconds later, a familiar-looking man with a folder in his hand entered the room and stood next to her. *The bushy beard guy from yesterday.* Except today he'd cleaned up and wore a fitted, navy-colored suit. Still had a beard, but he looked much younger than he did yesterday.

"You remember Agent Vargas from yesterday, right?" Deidra said.

Vargas extended his hand to me. "Richard Vargas, sir," he said.

I looked at his hand, then stared at him.

He pulled his hand back.

"What's going on?" I asked, turning my attention to Deidra.

She sighed and sat in the chair. "Mr. Black, you've single-handedly halted months of investigative work."

"I'm working undercover," Vargas said. "Those guys you saw me fighting were my way in."

"Your way into what? The hospital?" I said.

"I could've taken them."

"Not from where I was standing."

"Either way," Deidra said. "You've stalled our investigation, and you're gonna help get us back on track."

"And why would I do that? I was only trying to help an innocent civilian."

"Richard is a government agent. He was working a case that your actions hindered. That's called obstruction."

"You know that won't stick."

Deidra leaned back in the chair and folded her arms. "Maybe, maybe not. But it'd be a lot easier on you if you just cooperate," she said while tapping her biceps with her fingers.

I stared at her for a moment. We locked eyes, and she glanced away briefly before looking at me again and forcing a smile.

Someone's uneasy. "Cooperate how?"

Deidra's eyebrows rose, and she unfolded her arms. "So, you're going to play ball? Good choice."

"Just tell me what's going on."

"Right to business. I like it," she said before looking at Vargas and opening her hand.

Vargas gave her the folder he carried.

Deidra opened the folder, placed it on the table near me, and pointed to a man's head shot. "This is Christopher Navarro," she said.

He had smooth, tan skin, dimples, and combed-back hair. His picture should have been on a modeling agent's desk instead of a table inside of a government agency.

"He's part of the Escarra cartel," Deidra said.

"The cartel, great. Sounds like a fun bunch," I said under my breath.

"What's that?"

"Nothing."

"Okay. Well, as you can imagine, they're into drugs, human, and gun trafficking. All the crimes fitting of a cartel."

I sighed. "Yeah, that's what cartels do."

"This one takes part in somewhat of an... unusual activity. At least as far as cartels go."

I shrugged. "Let me guess, it's underground fighting?"

"Yes, you catch on quickly. Navarro is his cartel's representative for these organized fight groups. We were planting Vargas inside the organization. That is, before you obstructed his efforts."

"So now you want me to infiltrate the organization as a

fighter? And for my troubles, I won't be charged with obstruction."

Deidra's eyes widened and her lips parted. "Sharp. You really do understand."

I shook my head. "No. There's a lot I don't understand." *Like why are you willing to stoop so low just to make this case?* "Why is the DEA investigating underground fights? If you know Navarro is involved with running drugs, bust him on that. I mean... Drug Enforcement Administration, the word drug is in the agency's name."

"It's a process," Deidra said before closing the folder and handing it to Vargas.

"Right."

She stood from the table. "Come with me. I want to show you something."

I stood and followed her and Vargas out of the room.

"I'll catch up with you later," Vargas told Deidra, on our exit.

"Alright," she said before looking at me. "C'mon, this way."

We walked through the center of the office floor and into another room that housed three desks. Two were empty, and Jessica stood at the third with a document in hand. Near the back of the room, a paper-littered table sat flush with the wall. And at the far back wall stood an investigative board.

Deidra walked to the desk across from Jessica's. "Look who decided to play ball," she said to her.

Jessica smiled and looked at me. "Really? Welcome to the madness."

I shrugged but said nothing.

"Give me just a second, Mr. Black. Make yourself comfortable," Deidra said as she sat at her desk. She nodded toward a small room to my left. "If you want more coffee, there's some in the break room."

I walked toward the back of the room. On my way, I

noticed a picture on the third desk. In the picture was Vargas with a woman, a boy, and a girl. *Must be his family*, I thought as I continued to the investigative board.

The board had a few pictures, and marker-drawn lines connected them. There was a picture of Navarro with the words Escarra Cartel written below it. To the right of the picture was a face I'd never seen before with Ramos Cartel written at the bottom. Both pictures had lines drawn to a pair of images above them. In those pictures were the two guys I saw Vargas fighting with earlier. The image with the blond spiky-haired man had the name Ethan Long written next to it, and his partner with the short brown hair had the name Kody Snyder written next to his. Both their pictures had a line connecting them to a question mark drawn inside of a circle at the top of the board.

"Getting familiar with the case, Mr. Black?" Deidra said, approaching me.

"Not sure what I'm looking at, and you can stop calling me Mr.," I said.

"This is what I wanted to show you. Some faces should look familiar," she said as she stepped to the board.

"I recognize a few of them."

"We need to figure out who this is," she said, pointing at the question mark on the board. "This person is the reason the DEA is investigating an underground fighting ring. Whoever he is, he's in charge of the fight club and is supplying multiple cartels with drugs and financing."

"What's your plan for getting me in?" I asked.

"Vargas has some contacts to get you started with some small fights. From there, you'll work your way up to the high-profile fights where the big fish are."

"This sounds like it'll take a while."

Deidra shook her head. "That all depends on how good of a show you put on."

I stared at her.

"According to our intel, there will be a big fight in three days. They're looking for a challenger for the current champion. Lots of money involved, so we're positive whoever's pulling the strings will be there. I'd like to get you in that fight."

"Three days? It's going to take at least a week to prep and train."

Deidra shook her head again. "We don't have a week. We're working on getting your first fight later this afternoon."

"What? Are you tryin' to get me killed?"

"Don't be so dramatic, Black. I've read your file and seen you fight. This will be a cakewalk for you."

"I'm not worried about the fighting, but what about the cartels and this well-connected supplier?"

"Let us worry about that."

I stared at her again, but this time harder.

"Don't worry. We got you covered, you know?" she said before biting her bottom lip.

"We need more time, or this may come back to haunt us."

"We're ready now, and you have no choice."

"What if I don't win my fights?"

Deidra paused for a moment and inhaled before exhaling a shaky breath. "I'm not worried about that, because I know you can handle yourself. But if you happen to lose… well, the obstruction charges will be waiting for you."

"So, I basically get nothing for my efforts?"

"Sorry, Black, but failure is not an option here."

"There's something you're not telling me, but it'll all come out. I have a way of getting to the bottom of things."

Deidra forced a smile. "Well then, it should be easy for you to figure out who's our big question mark. C'mon, I'll explain more on the way to pick up your car."

I followed Deidra toward the front of the office. She stopped at Jessica's desk on the way.

"I believe we now have Mr. Black's full cooperation. I'm taking him to get his car," she told her partner.

Jessica squinted. "Are you sure? You don't want me to come?" she asked.

Deidra looked at me. "No, I'll be fine. I think we have an understanding, right, Black?"

I looked at her and shook my head. "Whatever," I said as I brushed past her and walked toward the door.

It took Deidra and me four minutes to make it downstairs and to the parking garage. Three minutes after that, we were on the road with her behind the wheel and me in the front passenger's seat. I was looking outside of my window at some road construction when I heard Deidra's voice.

"This won't be as bad as you think, Black," she said.

I looked at her and felt my eyebrows furrow as I did.

She glanced at me before looking back at the road. "We'll have your back, and it's not like you can't handle yourself."

"You're not very convincing," I said as I turned to my window and watched the trees and buildings roll by.

Deidra sighed. "We'll keep your car at HQ and set you up in a motel, you know, so you can maintain your cover."

I shrugged. "Whatever."

"Black, I'm gonna need you to get your head in the game."

"You act like you're paying me for this or something."

"Not charging you is payment. You don't have much of a choice."

"If you say so."

Deidra looked at me before shaking her head, then facing the windshield. "You should know these monsters have ruined many people's lives. Innocent people. Some—some really good people. I will not let them get away with it," she said with her eyes focused on the road.

I shrugged and looked out my window for the rest of the short, quiet drive. When we arrived at the hotel's parking lot, Deidra parked the sedan next to my Viper. I slid out of the sedan and circled to my car. As I did, Deidra rolled down her window.

"Stay close behind me," she said.

"Yeah, yeah. I got it," I said as I entered the Viper and started the engine.

Deidra pulled out of the parking lot, and I followed her back to the DEA's headquarters. We veered into the driveway, and she stopped at the security hut and exchanged some words with the guard. A moment later, the guard waved both of us through. We parked in the garage, entered the building together, and rode the elevator up to the fifth floor before walking to her office. Inside, both Jessica and Vargas sat at their desks.

Vargas stood with a sheet of paper in hand. "There you are," he said while walking to Deidra and me. He handed Deidra the paper. "I managed to get him in this fight. It's a small one, but there may be some big players there."

Deidra glanced down at the document and smiled. "Good work," she said.

"And his motel room is all ready," Jessica said as she stood and walked to us.

"Great. Let's iron out the details."

"Please do," I said.

Everyone looked at me.

"I'm the one who's going in. The one whose life is on the line, but I know the least about this plan I never agreed to."

Deidra sighed. "Black, your part is simple. Just put on a great show and gather any information that'll help us identify the question mark," she said, pointing at the investigative board in the back. "We have places where you can meet us or leave a message regarding your progress or any concerns you have."

"Also, there's this," Jessica said, walking back to her desk. She removed a flip phone and charger from her drawer. "This phone is programmed for secure communication. Deidra is your primary contact for this operation, so when you call her, the line will be encrypted. And the phone won't hold any information about the call, but it only does that for her phone number, so you'll have to memorize it." She handed me the phone and charger.

"Alright. That shouldn't be a problem," I said, while placing both the phone and charger in my pocket.

Deidra walked to her desk, grabbed a pen, and wrote on a sticky note before walking back and giving it to me. "This is my number. Like Jessica said, memorize it."

I looked at the number, committed it to memory, and handed the paper back to her. It took all of three seconds.

"Got it?" she asked.

"Really?"

She folded her arms and cocked her head to the side.

I sighed as I removed the flip phone from my pocket and dialed the number. The phone rang twice before Deidra's pocket buzzed.

She removed her phone and tapped at it. "Hello," she said into it.

I heard her through the phone and said, "I got it," before ending the call and jabbing the flip phone back into my pocket.

Deidra rolled her eyes and did the same with her phone. "Okay, you have an excellent memory. Should make things easier since I won't have to repeat myself. The first important detail you need to remember is, for the duration of this operation, you're not Orlando Black. You'll be Anthony White."

"That's original."

"As mentioned, you'll be put up in a motel, and that'll be your home. We'll provide you with money for food, personal care, and any other items you may need for this operation. Contact me anytime if you need something."

Vargas went to his desk and returned with another sheet of paper. "Here's a couple of addresses where you can leave us a message if things get sticky, or the phone stops working or you can't reach us. They're within walking distance of the motel."

I took the paper and memorized the locations before handing it back to him.

"At each spot there's a mailbox—which isn't really a mailbox, but you can drop your message in there. We'll be checking them periodically if we don't hear from you. But this is just in case of an emergency."

"And if you have to use this method of contact," Deidra said, "make sure you're not followed."

I shrugged. "Right."

"Also, anything that can identify you as Orlando Black, you'll have to leave here."

"Speaking of which. What about the two guys you were fighting, Vargas? Long and Snyder? Won't they recognize me?"

Vargas shook his head. "You were so fast. I don't think they remember what you looked like. When we talked after, neither one could describe you in any detail."

I nodded. "That may be true but seeing someone more than once could raise suspicion."

"He's right," Deidra said.

"Okay, what do you have in mind?" Vargas asked.

Deidra's eyes traced from my feet to the top of my head. "Black, how do you normally keep your hair?"

"It's usually a low-fade," I said. "But haven't had a cut or shave in a couple of weeks."

"More like over a month. But don't worry, the agency will take care of it for you, in-house."

"Good idea, but I don't let just anyone cut my hair."

"You mean you want a barber experienced in cutting black men's hair?"

"Suffice it to say, I don't wanna be walking around with a soup bowl."

Deidra laughed.

Jessica's eyebrows knitted. "What's a soup bowl?" she asked.

"I wouldn't do you like that, Black," Deidra said. "Don't worry, this guy has years of experience cutting hair like yours."

Anson entered the room as Deidra was speaking.

"I was just talking about you," she said.

"Are we ready?" Anson asked.

"Almost, but we'll need you to give Black a cut."

I stepped to Deidra's side. "Are you serious?" I whispered in her ear.

"Trust me, he's good," she whispered back.

"Well, c'mon, kid," Anson said while waving me over. "I don't have all day."

As I walked toward the door, I heard Deidra giggling behind me. I turned and looked at her and smiled, then followed Anson out of the office. We walked across the busy office floor, down a hall, then into a ten-by-fifteen room. As I entered, I felt a slight drop in temperature and a citrus aerosol fragrance struck my nose. Inside, a countertop occupied by clippers, trimmers, shavers, and cosmetic products ran the length of the room. Hanging above the countertop were three mirrors equally spaced along the wall. Three swivel chairs sat in front of each mirror, and on the opposite side of the room rested a sink, dryer, and a small table where more cosmetics lay.

"Well, take a seat," Anson said while pointing toward the swivel chairs.

I walked to the chair closest to the back and sat.

Anson met me there before turning me toward the mirror, opening a drawer under the counter, and removing an apron. He flapped the apron and threw it around me.

"So how long have you've been cutting hair?" I asked him.

Anson picked up a set of clippers. "Too long. Almost as long as I've been with the agency," he said, before spraying the blades with some type of aerosol disinfectant.

"How long have you been with the agency?"

"Twenty-nine years. Twenty-five of those years I've cut hair."

"That is a long time."

Anson used a towel to wipe the blades. "How do you want your hair?" he asked.

I looked at him in the mirror. "You know how to do a low-fade?"

"I sure do. My partner wore a low-fade, and I used to cut his hair all the time."

"Used to?"

"Yeah. He was killed on duty two years ago."

"Sorry to hear that."

"It happens."

"Given your seniority, I take it you're in charge of this operation."

Anson sighed. "No. I'm just support. My sight and hearing isn't what it used to be. I wouldn't be much help in the field."

"So, Deidra is running the show?"

Anson sighed again. "Yeah. I've tried to get her to hand it off to someone else, but she's stubborn."

"I noticed."

Anson chuckled. "I bet you have," he said while picking up a comb and sliding it through my hair.

"Why'd you want her to hand it off?"

"Enough talking," Anson said with a grunt. "Be still or you may end up looking like a leopard."

I sat still and quiet with many questions in my head while Anson flipped on the clippers.

. . .

Forty-five minutes later, Anson used the towel to wipe the loose hair from around my neck and flapped the apron from around me. I looked into the mirror and saw someone I hadn't seen in two weeks, or over a month, if I let Deidra tell it. I turned to my right side, then my left.

"You did a really good job. Thanks," I said.

"Like I said, I've been doing it for quite some time," Anson said as he walked to the back corner and grabbed a broom and dustpan.

I stood from the chair and further inspected myself in the mirror, and as I did, the door swung open and Jessica entered.

"They need to see you back in the office," she said to me, slightly out of breath.

CHAPTER
FOUR

"OKAY, WHAT'S GOING on?" I asked.

"I'll explain on the way," Jessica said.

I walked through the door and into the hall.

Jessica smiled as I passed her. "You look even cuter with a haircut," she said before looking back at Anson. "We'll fill you in."

Jessica and I walked back to the office and found Deidra and Vargas standing near Deidra's desk.

"There you are," she said as she examined my haircut. "It looks good."

"Thanks," I said.

She handed me two sheets of paper. "Here, memorize this. It's your new identity. Your fight's been moved up an hour, so we're gonna have to move."

"I'll go change my clothes," Vargas said on his way toward the door.

I looked at the document and saw a picture of me with the name Anthony White next to it. Apparently, I grew up in Connecticut as a troubled youth and went to prison for armed robbery and attempted murder.

"You got it?" Deidra asked me.

I nodded. "Yeah, the gist of it."

"Black, I need you to have it down."

"I will if I can have more than five seconds to review the cover," I said, walking toward the back of the office.

As I continued to review my cover dossier, Deidra and Jessica stood whispering. It appeared Deidra was giving out orders until she tilted her head back on an inhale, then hung it toward the floor on an exhale.

Jessica placed a hand on her colleague's shoulder. "It'll be okay," she said.

Deidra lifted her head and nodded.

"Okay then, I'm going downstairs to get the car ready," Jessica said before leaving the office.

On her exit, Anson entered and went to Deidra.

"Is everything okay?" he asked.

"Yeah. Just they moved the match up an hour and I..."

Anson placed his hand on her shoulder. "We're going to get them, don't worry."

"I know."

"Come here," Anson said before pulling Deidra toward him for a quick embrace. "Just follow the plan," he said as he nudged her to arm's length.

Deidra nodded.

"I'm here if you need anything," he said on his way out the door.

As Deidra turned to me, I looked at the papers as if I didn't hear or see anything that took place.

She approached me. "So, do you have it now?"

I gave her the dossier. "All of it."

"Here," she said, reaching into her pocket and producing a driver's license.

I took it. It was a Texas license with my picture, cover name and the usual information on it.

Deidra sighed. "Okay, Orlando Black, let's get you downstairs. Your ride is in the parking garage."

"Who?" I said.

Deidra stared at me as wrinkles crossed her forehead. "Oh, very good," she said with a slight chuckle. "I was just testing you. Let's go, Mr. Anthony White."

When Deidra and I made it to the parking garage, I went to my car and opened the passenger's side door. I took some cash out of my wallet and stuffed the bills into my pocket before placing the wallet into my glove compartment. I locked the car, then walked to Deidra.

"I don't want to see a single scratch on my car," I said, handing her my keys.

She tilted her head. "Don't worry, it'll be safe here. I won't let anything happen to your precious car."

I stared at her.

"I promise nothing will happen to your car," she said again. "Do you have anything else on you?"

I knelt and lifted my right pants' hem, exposing one of my dual knife holsters strapped around my ankle. "Just these. But they stay with me."

Deidra shook her head. "I don't know, Black."

"I'll take them off before my fight. Plus, it won't hurt to have a little extra protection while undercover. Having knives won't raise a lot of suspicion for a guy like Anthony White, but him not having any weapons at all, just might."

"Fine, you can keep them. I doubt it'll hurt your cover—just be careful."

"Always."

Deidra parted her lips to speak, but before she could, the rev of an engine flowed from behind me. I turned to find Jessica sitting at the wheel of a dented, silver Ford Focus. She winked at me before parking and exiting the car.

"Your ride's here," she said.

I smiled. "Will it make it?"

Jessica shrugged. "Vargas has a... modest cover."

I shook my head and circled to the front of the car. The

hood needed a fresh coat of paint. The headlights were fogged, and the windshield cracked.

As I continued inspecting, Deidra and Jessica chitchatted. I paid little attention to what was being said because the bald tires on the Focus had my attention. I kept my eyes on the front passenger's side tire until I heard Vargas' voice. He wore blue jeans and a wrinkled black shirt as he approached Deidra and Jessica.

"Are we ready?" he asked.

Deidra looked at me. "Are you ready, Black?"

I shrugged. "You haven't given me much of a choice, so yeah, I guess I am."

She exhaled, and the energy drained from her face as she stared at me.

"Well, let's go," Vargas said, opening the driver's side door.

I did the same on the passenger's side before looking back at Deidra. "Was there something else you wanted to tell me?"

She shook her head.

I hunched my shoulders and joined Vargas inside the car, where the scent of vanilla fused with exhaust struck my nose.

"You boys be careful," Jessica said as Vargas put the car in gear and cruised out of the parking garage.

Two minutes later, we were on the highway.

Vargas looked at me. "Black, I'm glad you're on the team."

I winced. "Team? You realize my hand was forced, right?"

"It's nothing personal. It's just this case means a lot to Deidra."

"I can see that—I want to know why."

Vargas shrugged. "It's complicated, not sure I completely understand myself."

I shook my head before turning to my window to watch the power lines and houses roll by.

"What about you?" I asked, still looking out of my window. "Why is this case so important to you?"

"It's my job," Vargas said with a chuckle. "These people are involved in some bad stuff, and I want to stop them. Plus, after working undercover for nearly two months, I'm feeling really vested."

I looked at Vargas as he stared through the windshield. He seemed honest. I believed what he told me but knew there was something even deeper motivating him to close this case.

"How often do you see your family?" I asked.

He glanced at me before looking back at the road. "Not often enough," he said with a sigh. "But anyhow. From this moment forward, you're no longer Orlando Black."

"Got it. I'm Anthony White."

"Exactly. And I'm Hector Corrales," Vargas said before coughing, then buzzing his window down.

"You okay?" I asked.

"Yeah, just this exhaust smell can get strong on the driver's side." Vargas pointed at a small, yellow paper tree hanging from the interior rear-view mirror. "I put this car freshener in to help, and it does, but sometimes the smell is overpowering."

I buzzed down my window.

"But yeah, I'm Hector Corrales, and I met you at a bar last night. A fight broke out and you handled yourself well, so I thought you'd be the perfect contender."

"That's it?"

"Yeah, pretty much. We don't know a lot about each other. I'll let them look into your background themselves. The tech guys at the agency are great with setting up covers, so you'll be fine as long as you know your cover story front and back. You memorized it, right?"

"I did."

"Good. And you have the driver's license for your cover?"

"I do."

"We should be all set, then."

"What's the name of the bar?"

Vargas squinted at me. "What?"

"The bar where we met. What's the name of it?"

"Oh, it's called the Snake Pit. And there was an actual bar fight there last night."

"Do you know the owner?"

"Some guy who goes by the name Big Dale."

"Was he there last night?"

"Yes, our sources confirm he was. Good questions. You really wanna sell this, huh?"

"I really wanna stay alive."

"Don't worry about that. We got you covered."

I looked at him. "Do you?"

Vargas glanced at me. "Of course we do. I know Deidra can be tough, but she wouldn't really—" he said before briefly locking eyes with me. "She won't let anything happen to you," he finished, while facing the windshield.

"I'm not worried about anything happening to me."

"Seems like it."

I shook my head. "Just being careful. Being careful keeps you alive. Worrying doesn't. And if at any point I feel you guys aren't being careful with this operation, I'll leave and you'll never see me again."

Vargas stared at me.

I stared back. "Yeah, those little charges Deidra threatened me with…not worried about 'em."

"Then why would you go through with this?"

"I don't like things lingering over me. You know, unfinished business. And I'm partly responsible for *obstructing* your investigation. Don't like to leave things a mess. Plus, something about this case has really piqued my interest."

"Piqued your interest? This is not a field trip. These are dangerous people, Black."

"I know that. But they're still just people. Which means they have strengths, weaknesses, things they love, and things they hate. We have to be careful and patient enough to learn what they are; if we want the mission to be a success."

"As simple as that, huh? Easy peasy."

"No, people at their core are simple, but this won't be easy."

We drove for another couple of miles before turning onto a poorly paved side road. The Focus hummed up the road for another mile where Vargas made a right turn onto a dirt road. In the distance, I saw a few hangars surrounded by a fence.

"Is this an airport?" I asked.

Vargas nodded at the wheel. "It's an old, abandoned airport, and one venue for these low-level fights."

As we made it closer to the old airport, Vargas slowed. The chain-linked fence rolled by on our right with signs that warned us we were on private property and shouldn't trespass. Twenty-five yards ahead I saw a gated entrance. Standing on either side of the entrance were two muscular men.

Vargas looked at me. "Don't forget, I'm Hector Corrales and you're Anthony White. Remember your cover and how we met," he said, concern in his voice. "And let me do all the talking."

I shrugged.

Vargas made a right turn, then stopped the car before pushing the gearshift into park.

The two men approached. One on Vargas' side and the other on mine. The man approaching Vargas had messy hair and was shorter than his partner. I watched as the guy on my side stared at me through the window before he scratched his buzzed hair and inspected the inside of the car.

Vargas rolled down his window. "Hi Juan, what's up?"

Juan fixed on Vargas' face and squinted. As he stepped closer to the car, he smiled. "Que pasa, Hector. Haven't seen you in a minute."

"Yeah, been busy, tryna' hustle."

"I hear ya—I hear ya."

The guy on my side, the one with the buzz cut, walked past my window. As he did, I saw the butt of a gun tucked in his front waistband. It was a Smith & Wesson 5906. Weight, about thirty-eight ounces. Magazine capacity, fifteen rounds. Well made and rarely jammed. All in all, a great firearm. But considering its jagged design, it may not be the best handgun to have tucked in your pants.

"So, you here to fight?" Juan asked Vargas.

"No, no, I'm not competing."

"You know what? I heard you got whupped by those soft white boys—the ones that the higher-ups sent to recruit."

"I was—there was two of 'em…"

Juan laughed. "It's okay, man," he said, while arching down and patting Vargas on the shoulder. "You know them boys ain't gonna let you sit at their table. Stick with these smaller fights. We gotcha." He looked at me. "Who's this?"

Vargas glanced at me and said, "He's a fighter."

Juan looked me up and down. "Okay, what's your name, Mr. Fighter?"

"White, Anthony White," I said.

"You look like you're in shape, but that doesn't mean much. Are you any good?"

"Is he," Vargas cut in. "I saw him beat two guys like it was nothing."

"Really? Is that true? You can beat two men at once?"

I shrugged. "Maybe even more."

Juan laughed, then stood from the car as the man with the buzz cut approached him.

"It looks clean. Just need to check the trunk," he told Juan before looking at Vargas. "Pop the trunk."

Vargas reached for the trunk's latch.

Juan gestured for him to stop. "Nah, don't worry about it. Hector's good, man. Ya'll go'on through," he said.

"See ya around, Juan," Vargas said.

"Fo'sho. And Mr. Fighter," Juan said, bending down and looking at me. "Good luck."

I shrugged and faced the windshield.

Juan laughed and stood from the car. "Go'on through," he said, patting the hood of the Focus.

Vargas dragged the gear stick to drive, and we pulled off. Clouds of dust encompassed the car as we drove across the dirt. The car rocked along the path for two minutes until we reached the tarmac. We passed two small hangars on our way to a larger one near the back. The large sliding doors were open and nearly twenty cars sat parked around the hangar.

"Quite the turnout for a small fight," I said.

"Sometimes it's even more people than this," Vargas said.

We parked just off the tarmac, somewhat away from the other cars. Vargas exited the car first. When I exited, I circled to his side and we walked toward the front sliding doors. Chanting and hip-hop music flowed from inside. At the front stood a tall, bulky man with his arms folded and a mean look on his face. He nodded at Vargas as if he knew him, then gestured for us to enter the hangar. The smell of nicotine stuffed the air, and a crowd surrounded a mat at the center of the hangar. Everyone in the mob was shouting, clapping, or fist pumping.

"Looks like the first match has already started," Vargas said.

We threaded through the crowd until we found a spot where we could observe the fight. On the mat, two men dressed in jeans and t-shirts threw wild punches and kicks at each other. I shook my head at how sloppy and unintentional their attacks were. Even the referee shook his head while keeping his distance as the two men duked it out.

Vargas looked at me. "What?" he asked, wide eyed. "Are you concerned?"

I scoffed. "No."

"Okay. Just making sure. This type of fighting is very barbaric and can intimidate even the best of fighters."

"I'll be fine. Trust me."

"Let's get you checked in."

We weaved through the horde of people and to the back of the hangar, where there was a booth. Behind the window stood a stocky man with missing teeth.

"Hector, long time no see," the man said as we approached.

"Yeah, I've been busy," Vargas said.

"Busy doing what? Tryna' enter the high-ticket circuit?"

Vargas hunched his shoulders but said nothing.

The man behind the window chuckled. "It's okay. We won't hold it against you. I heard your try-outs didn't go too well though."

"News sure travels fast."

"That's the business. So, are you here to fight?"

Vargas shook his head. "Oh no, I'm not," he said before looking at me. "But I do have a fighter."

The stocky man craned toward the window and looked me up and down. His nose crinkled, and he shrugged. "I've seen plenty of fighters come through here and this one's hard to read. Is he any good?"

"He's better than good," Vargas said.

"Okay. What's your name, fighter?" the man asked me.

"White, Anthony White," I said.

The man's lips protruded, and he kissed the few teeth he had. "Okay, White. You're up next. You'll have fifteen minutes to get ready. Lockers and warm-up equipment is in the back," he said before looking at Vargas. "How much are you putting on your fighter, Hector?"

"Three stacks," Vargas said.

The stocky man's eyes widened. "Three grand? Are you sure? That's a lot to put up for a walk-in. Especially when he's fighting against Butch."

Vargas' eyebrows knitted. "Wait-wait-wait, Butch is here? He's one of the best fighters in this circuit."

The heavy-set guy nodded. "I know," he said while looking down and writing.

"Okay, well, maybe we should hold off until a later match."

"Sorry Hector, you know the rules. I've already filled out the paperwork and this is the only match I can get him in." The man slid a piece of paper under the window.

Vargas looked at me and sighed before reaching into his pocket, removing a wad of bills, and sliding them under the window.

"Thank you," the man said with a grin. "You got about fifteen minutes to get ready while the current fight finishes, and I get the bets in for your match."

"Yeah, we heard you the first time," Vargas said to the man before turning to me. "This way."

We walked toward a hall, and as we did, Vargas hung his head and his eyes wandered.

"Something you want to share with me?" I asked.

Vargas lifted his head and looked around before stepping closer to me. "Butch is a good fighter, Black."

"Yeah, so?"

"I-I think you can beat him, but if you get hurt, you'll need time to recover—"

"And I wouldn't be ready for the big fight in three days," I said.

"Exactly."

"I guess I better not get hurt then."

Vargas took in a breath, then exhaled slowly. "The restroom and equipment is this way," he said while walking down the hall.

I followed him to the end of the hall where we made a left past a concrete partition and into a room. Inside were lockers, sinks, benches, showers, weights, and punching bags.

"What do you need to get ready?" Vargas asked me.

I shrugged. "Not much. Do they have any toilets here?"

"Yeah, at the back, make a right," Vargas said while pointing.

I walked to the back of the room and made a right into a section with four urinals and two toilet stalls. I used the urinal, then walked back to the locker area and washed my hands. Vargas was still standing there.

"So, are you good?" he asked me.

"I'm fine. Why don't you sit down and relax?" I said.

Vargas took a seat on a bench.

I removed the flip phone and my ankle knife holsters and gave them to him. "Hold on to these."

Vargas eyed the knives. "Where did these come from?"

"Just make sure I get them back after the fight."

"Sure, whatever."

I rotated my hips, then tilted my neck from side-to-side before arching and touching my toes. I saw Vargas staring at me as I performed lunges.

"Is there an issue?" I asked.

Vargas shook his head and looked away.

"Just relax," I said to him before throwing a few jabs and kicks at the punching bag.

I concluded my warm-ups by raising my arms above my head on a long inhale, then circling them down with a slow exhale. I did this ten times.

"Okay, I'm ready," I said to Vargas.

He winced at me. "That's it?"

"That's it. Just wanted to loosen my body a little."

"Are you sure?"

"Positive. Now let's go."

We left the locker room and walked through the crowd toward the mat. The referee stood at the center, watching as we approached. When we reached the corner of the mat, Vargas tapped my shoulder.

"Wait here until the ref calls you on the mat," he said.

I nodded.

I looked to the opposite corner and saw a guy with a wide head and muscular frame sporting a red wife-beater and dark-blue jeans. The man threw a few jabs at the air.

"That's Butch," Vargas said. "Like I told you, he's a good fighter. I'm sure most everyone put their money on him. So, what do you think? You think you can beat him?"

I watched as Butch continued to throw jabs and noticed he always dropped his left arm after throwing a jab with it. "Don't worry. I got it," I said to Vargas.

"Okay."

A woman stepped onto the mat and handed the referee a microphone. She caught a lot of the men's eyes on her way and held them as she stood next to the referee.

The ref put the microphone to his lips, and the speakers scratched as he looked and pointed in my direction. "In the black corner we have a new challenger," he started. "He has no fight history and goes by the name White."

Over half the crowd booed.

"Yeah, I don't like that name either," the referee said. "I think we'll call him… um… Ghost!"

"That sounds about right," a man from the crowd shouted. "Because that's what Butch's gonna make him." The man laughed.

I glanced at Vargas. "Friendly crowd," I said under my breath.

The referee then pointed to Butch. "In the red corner, we have one of the top contenders in this circuit. The man slaying, wild animal taming, Butch!"

Butch threw his hands in the air, and most of the crowd cheered.

"Fighters, step on the mat."

Both Butch and I walked to the center. The woman stepped back as we approached the referee. He dropped the microphone to his side and looked at both of us as we stared at each other.

"Make this a good fight. No dirty low-blows, no eye-gouging, no biting. Remember to protect yourself at all times. Break."

I walked back to my corner, and Butch did the same. Once there, Butch slid into a fighting stance and raised his fists. I didn't bother to. The referee then pointed at Butch, and he nodded. He did the same to me, and I nodded.

"Let's fight!" he shouted into the microphone before handing it to the woman, who quickly exited the mat.

I walked about five feet from my corner before Butch raced toward me. I stepped back a foot to keep him at jabbing distance, then waited. Butch threw a right punch, and I parried it. He then followed up with the attack I was waiting for. A left jab. I bobbed under the punch and ended up on his left side, and just as I expected, he dropped his arm. I delivered a hard hook to his left jaw, and he collapsed to the mat. The cheers and yells from the crowd died, and the hangar went completely silent as I turned and walked off the mat.

Vargas' mouth hung open with the whites of his eyes exposed.

I patted him on the shoulder. "Hey, let's go."

He broke out of his trance, and we threaded through the mob with wide eyes staring at us. The speakers scratched and the referee's voice came through.

"Ah... and the winner of this fight by knockout, Ghost!"

The hangar remained silent as Vargas and I walked toward the back booth. As we approached, the stocky man with the missing teeth shook his head.

"I... I don't believe it," he said. "The fight is already over?"

Vargas grinned. "Yep, and I believe you owe me some money. What were the odds?"

The man sighed. "Most bets were on Butch, but we can only do a max of twenty-five to one."

"So three thousand times twenty-five. That's seventy-five thousand."

The man grunted. "I can count, Hector," he said before squatting behind the booth and fiddling with what sounded like keys.

A few moments later, the man stood with a bag and eight stacks of bills.

"Ten, twenty, thirty, forty, fifty, sixty, seventy, five," the stocky man counted as he placed the stacks inside the bag.

He then dropped the bag in a compartment to his right and pushed a lever. A chute door opened on our side, and Vargas grabbed the bag.

"Nice doing business with you," he said to the man.

"Yeah, whatever," the man said. "Hey fighter, who are you?" he asked me as Vargas and I turned to leave.

I looked over my shoulder. "I already told you. Anthony White."

"Yeah, but who are you?"

"Let's just stick with what the ref called me: Ghost," I said before following Vargas out of the hangar.

CHAPTER
FIVE

"YOU SHOULD'VE SEEN him, Deidra," Vargas said into his wireless ear piece as he veered the Focus onto the highway. "He knocked out a top contender with one punch."

I glanced at him and shook my head as I finished strapping my knife holster around my ankle.

"Never seen anything like it," Vargas continued. He listened for a few moments. "No, no, I haven't heard from anyone yet, but everyone there was speechless." Vargas paused again and listened. "Yeah, we're on our way to the motel now. ... Sure, I'll let you know when I'm headed back. ... Of course, I'll be bringing the earnings back with me. ... Alright, talk to you then, bye." He ended the call and looked at me with an enormous grin. "Things are off to a great start."

I said nothing.

"Don't you think?" Vargas asked.

"Maybe. You said Butch was one of the best fighters in this circuit. Do you know if he's ever fought in the high-ticket matches?"

Vargas shook his head. "I don't believe he has," he said with his eyes on the road.

"So, they don't believe he's good enough for it?"

"Getting into those matches is political. It's about money. Although he's not on your level, Butch is a great fighter for this circuit, but he still has that thug-like demeanor."

"So, they're looking for someone who fights well, but with a certain elegance."

"Exactly."

"Seems it'll be hard for them to find someone like that in this circuit. The fighters I've seen so far are rough around the edges, unpolished."

"Well, that's certainly not you. I'm sure word about your performance today will get back to them fast."

"That's what I'm afraid of," I said under my breath.

"What's that?"

"Nothing."

Vargas glanced at me before shrugging, then placing his attention back on the road. We drove for another fifteen minutes before he turned off the main road and onto the motel's driveway. The motel was a two-story structure made of orange brick. The stairs and railing were white with chipped paint, and the parking lot was virtually empty. Including the Focus, there were only four cars in the entire lot. Vargas wheeled the car into a spot.

"Here's your new home. For the next few days at least," he said.

I said nothing, and continued to survey the area.

"I know it's not the Ritz-Carlton," Vargas continued. "But you'll be on the first level. Room 6A," he finished before handing me a key. "Remember Black, you're now Anthony White and I'm Hector Corrales."

"I got it."

"Just making sure. My number's programmed in the flip phone Jessica gave you earlier. It's under Hector, so when we're on the phone, we only talk about things that Anthony and Hector would talk about. Nothing concerning the operation. If you need to provide operation specific details—"

"Wait to talk with you in person or call Deidra's number that I memorized because the line will be encrypted," I interrupted.

"Right, and—"

"If things get really sticky or I can't reach you, leave a message in the mailbox at either of the locations that I also memorized. Got it."

Vargas sighed. "I just want to make sure we cover all of our bases."

"Understood."

Vargas dug into his pocket and produced a small wad of cash. "Here's some spending money, for food and what not."

I took the wad and stuffed it into my pocket. "Is that it? Are all the bases covered now?" I said.

Vargas nodded.

"Alright. I'll see you around," I said as I opened my door.

"You know what?" Vargas said. "I'll walk in with you, just to check out the room."

I shrugged. "Okay," I said before exiting the car and shutting the door.

The room was at the far west corner of the building. I inserted the key in the door and rotated it until I heard a click, then turned the knob and pushed the door open. Inside was a queen-size bed, a dresser with a television resting on top, a desk, and a microwave. Whoever made the bed made it without a single wrinkle in the comforter, and the faint scent of cleaning solution lingered in the air.

"Better than what I was expecting," I said.

"Yeah, they've been slowly renovating this building," Vargas said as he closed the door.

I looked down and noticed vinyl flooring running from the living area into the bathroom. "Definitely better than some motels I've seen."

Vargas walked to the bathroom briefly, and when he returned, he opened the dresser drawers and peeked inside each. One by one. "There's some change of clothes in the drawers. Mainly jeans and t-shirts. Should fit you. Oh, and there's some workout clothes just in case, you know, you wanna workout."

"Thanks."

Vargas scanned the room once more before walking to the door. "Alright, I'm out. I'll be in touch when I have your next fight. Be careful, Black."

I winced. "Black, who's that?"

Vargas chuckled on his way out. I closed, then locked the door behind him. The first thing I wanted to do was get a lay of the land, but before I did, I figured I'd make sure my current channel of communication was operational. I removed the phone from my pocket and flipped it open. The battery showed fully charged, and I was getting three bars of signal. *We're good there,* I thought as I opened the top dresser drawer. A new pack of boxer briefs, socks, and t-shirts lay inside. In the drawer below were jeans, and in the last drawer was some activewear, like Vargas said. The bathroom had all the linen I needed, and a box of toothpaste and a new toothbrush, sat on the counter next to the sink. *I guess the DEA is doing something right.*

I stepped out of the room, ensured the door locked shut, then walked to the opposite end of the motel. It was quiet, and I only saw one other person around the building. I looked up the road and noticed a sign for a diner about a quarter of a mile away. I walked in that direction, figuring it would be best to eat while I could. After walking the quarter of a mile, I came to an old one-story building with boarded doors and windows. A metal plaque with five numbers etched in it hung above the door. I recognized the number as one of the two addresses I memorized for the secure drop locations. I looked around and noticed a blue, rusted mail drop box with two locks on the back of it, bolted to a concrete foundation.

I shrugged. *Found one of 'em.*

The diner was twenty-five yards up the road on the opposite side of the highway. A small establishment with little parking, which was fine by me considering I didn't have a car. I pulled the door open, and a bell dinged as I entered. Directly in front of me sat a bar top with stools lined in front of it, and on the other side of the bar top, two cooks occupied the kitchen. One was heavy-set, and he looked at me as he wiped his hand across his apron.

"We'll be with you in a minute. Have a seat anywhere you like. Kelly!" he said.

I nodded and looked to my right. Booths ran the length of the restaurant all the way to the restroom at the end. To the left was the same, but instead of a bathroom at the end, there was an isolated booth. *Bingo.* I proceeded across the checkered tiled floor and the scent of burgers, fries, and ketchup hit my nose as I passed a family of four sitting in a booth. I nodded and the father and mother returned the gesture. As I sat at my booth, a door near the kitchen flapped open and a middle-aged woman with silky dirty-blonde hair entered the dining room. She rolled her eyes at the heavy-set cook before pacing over to me with a menu in hand.

"Evening, sir. My name is Kelly and I'll be serving you," she said, handing me the menu. "What can I start you off with to drink?"

I quickly glanced over the menu and considered a burger and fries but thought about it and decided on something a little more appropriate for my current situation. "I'll just have a water, and I know what I want," I said.

Kelly smiled. "Awesome. That was quick. So, what can I get for you?"

"I'll have your grilled chicken, brown rice, and steamed broccoli."

"Oh, the healthy choice."

"Yeah, trying to watch my figure."

Kelly smiled and glanced me over. "Your figure looks fine to me," she said while extending her hand.

I returned the smile and passed her the menu.

She tucked it under her arm. "I'll get that in for you, Mr...."

"White. Anthony White," I said.

Kelly smiled again. "Okay, Mr. White. I'll be back with your water."

I nodded then watched as she walked away and disappeared behind the same door she had entered. A minute later, she returned with a cup of water.

"There you go," she said as she sat it on the table. "Anything else?" she asked while placing a straw next to the cup.

"No, I think I'm good for now," I said.

Kelly returned to the kitchen and talked with the heavyset cook. The two exchanged words before she shook her head, threw a hand in the air, and walked through the door again.

I shrugged, then peeled the paper from my straw before dropping the straw into my cup and taking a sip. Before I could take a second sip, I felt a vibration in my pocket. The words *unknown number* displayed on the flip phone.

"Hello," I answered.

"Hi Black, this is Deidra. What are you doing? Can you talk?"

"Grabbing an early dinner. And yes, I can talk."

"Great. I spoke with Vargas today, and things are off to an excellent start. Great job."

"Thank you, I guess."

"You may not think so, but we're doing good work here."

"No, I believe these people are bad and need to be taken down. It's just the methods. Something's off, and I'll find out what it is. I always do."

The line with silent for a moment.

Deidra sighed. "I'm not sure what you're hoping to find, but I'm just doing my job here."

"I don't doubt that," I said, then immediately thought, *Just not sure of your motivations.*

"Okay then. Do you need anything or—"

"Nope."

"Well, enjoy your dinner and have a good evening. Make sure you get some rest. There's no telling when Vargas could have another fight lined up for you."

"Got it. Talk with you later."

"Bye."

I ended the call, placed the phone in my pocket, then sat with my thoughts for twenty minutes. During that time, the restaurant's population increased by fifty percent.

Kelly came to my table and set my plate down. "It smells good," she said. "I think I might have the same thing at the end of my shift."

"You always work this shift?" I asked.

"Yeah, but only for a few hours, so I'll be getting off soon."

"You like it here?"

Kelly shrugged. "It's okay, I guess. Just working here for a little extra money. During the day I work at the mall." She pointed. "Half a mile up the road. Then walk here to work for a few hours."

I nodded. "Busy day."

"It can be. Anything else I can get for you, Mr. White?" she asked.

"No, I'm okay for now, thanks."

"Okay, let me know if you need anything," she said with a smile before walking away toward a recently occupied booth.

It took me less than twenty minutes to clean my plate. I sat for a minute to let my food digest, then dropped enough cash on the table to cover the meal and leave Kelly a twenty-dollar tip. On my way out of the diner, she waved at me.

"Nice to meet you. Have a good night, bye."

I waved back and exited the diner.

The sun dipped toward the horizon and the sky was dark by the time I made it back to my room. I removed the contents of my pockets and placed them near the clock on the nightstand next to the bed. Figuring I better follow Deidra's advice and get some rest while I could, I took off my shoes, washed my hands and face, brushed my teeth, then plopped on the bed and closed my eyes.

When I opened them next, the clock displayed 4:30 a.m. I sat up and took in a deep breath before standing, stretching, then dropping to the floor and performing one hundred push-ups, followed by the same number of sit-ups. Once finished, I stood from the floor and shadow boxed, then performed some judo and wrestling drills I learned as a teenager. The clock now showed 5:42 a.m., and I wanted to conclude my workout with some form practice, but there wasn't enough room inside, so I threw on a sweatshirt and a pair of sweatpants and stepped outside into the darkness. At the end of the motel was a small, dimly lit field. Perfect for what I needed. I started with a karate form I learned as a kid, then a Shaolin Kung Fu form I learned during my time in China, and concluded with tai chi. After I went back to the room, showered, and dressed, the clock displayed 7:16 a.m., and I was thinking about breakfast.

I went back to the same diner where I ate the night before. Saw the same heavy-set cook in the kitchen. And sat at the same booth. It was practically the same experience except a freckled-faced young man in his early twenties served me. After my meal, I made the half-mile walk to the mall. It was a large, off-white building composed of various restaurants, clothing stores, and shops. I concluded it was the spot where everyone conducted their business because surrounding the mall were grocery stores, more restaurants, banks, and department stores. The cars in the mall's parking lot were sparse. I figured the mall was closed, so I walked across the street to a coffee shop and ordered a green tea despite my craving for a coffee. I sat with my cup and thought maybe I was too nice for jumping in and helping Vargas during his little audition. Sipping the tea, my mind went to the big fight that was now only two days away. I sighed, then seriously considered going back to the DEA HQ, getting into my car, and leaving town, but as I took another sip, I thought about all the innocent people the Cartels had hurt.

Yeah, too nice.

After sitting with my thoughts for another half hour, I left the coffee shop and headed across the street to the mall. The parking lot began to fill, and many people walked toward the building. I entered the mall through a sporting goods store and immediately a leather-rubbery scent hit my nose. As I walked past a rack of canoes and a rack of fishing rods and reels, I heard scraping coming from my right. A short man with gray on his face and head was pulling a pallet of boxes. When he saw me, he stopped, squinted, then walked toward me.

"How you doing, sir? Anything I can help you find?" he asked.

I shook my head. "No. Just looking around."

The man smiled. "Okay," he said, nodding his head. "Are you an outdoorsman?"

I shrugged. "Sometimes."

"What? Do you hunt?"

I nodded. "Yeah, I do a little hunting from time to time."

"Oh great! Now we don't sell guns in the store, but upstairs," the man said while pointing at some stairs, "we have a new selection of crossbows and bows and arrows."

"I may just have to check that out," I said.

"Okay, let me know if you need help with anything," he said on his way back to his pallet.

I continued through the store and out to the mall's main concourse. The sound of footsteps and voices immediately struck my ears. There was a shoe store to my left and a jewelry store to my right, and four yards in front of me, a young woman at a kiosk selling sunglasses to a woman wearing a strapless white and blue summer dress. I walked past and made a left where more stores flanked me on both sides. I counted six people walking ahead of me, two behind me, and a few entering and exiting the stores. It all reminded me why I really didn't enjoy going to malls. There were only a handful of people, but they were coming from multiple directions all at once. I could only imagine what it'd be like with the mall packed; threat detection would become a challenge.

I passed a playground area and into a food court where most of the restaurants were closed or just opening. After circling the food court, I walked back in the direction I came, past the hall for the sporting goods store and to the opposite side of the mall. It was more of the same. More shops, more kiosks, more people, and more headache for me. As I turned to leave, something caught my eye, or rather, someone. Kelly, the waitress from the morning before, stood outside of a shoe store, but she wasn't alone. Standing next to her was someone I'd seen two days prior. One of the men Vargas duked it out with, Ethan Long.

Whatta ya know.

I slipped behind a kiosk and pretended to admire the assortment of candles while watching the two converse from my peripheral. Long said something while Kelly shrugged and shook her head before saying something back with squinted eyes. Long hunched his shoulders, then Kelly shrugged again before pivoting toward the store and waving at him. He waved back before walking in my direction. I faced the shelf of candles and inhaled a vanilla scent while Long's footsteps knocked past me. The blond spiky-haired man continued down the concourse before making a left and disappearing from my sight.

I entered the shoe store and saw Kelly as she walked down the center aisle and to the back. As I strolled down the aisle, perusing the shelves on either side of me, a thin, young man with dark hair and pale skin approached me. He wore a black polo shirt with the store's logo embroidered on it.

"Anything I can help you with?" he asked.

"Naw, just looking," I said.

"Okay, I'll be at the register if you need anything."

I nodded, then walked to the men's section. A moment later, Kelly returned from the back wearing the same shirt as the store clerk. As she walked past me, I turned to a pair of boots, picked one up, and pretended to inspect it. She went to the register and had a word with her co-worker. The two laughed, and then she walked back in my direction. I sat the boot down and stepped into the center aisle as she was coming. Kelly paused as I glanced at her, smiled, then continued to the opposite side of the aisle.

"Excuse me," she said to my back.

I glanced over my shoulder and squinted as if I didn't recognize her.

"Hi," she said.

"Hey, hi, um…"

"I waited on you yesterday—at the diner."

"Right."

"Mr. White. Anthony, right?"

"Yeah, and you're Kelly, um… Long," I said, taking a shot in the dark at the last name.

She squinted and tilted her head. "I told you my last name?"

I shrugged, and she smiled.

"But yeah," she continued. "You always come to the mall this early? The store just opened like ten minutes ago." She smiled.

"I'm somewhat of an early bird."

"I'll say. You nearly beat me here."

"No, I think you got here before me. I saw you standing outside talking with your boyfriend," I said.

Kelly winced. "No, no, no. That was my older brother, Ethan."

You don't say. "Oh, sorry. My mistake."

"No worries. He's been hassling me about walking to work. Even offered to buy me a new car—my current car is in the shop."

"That's nice of him."

Kelly hunched her shoulders. "Yeah, but I like to do things on my own."

"You don't like owing anyone. I get that."

"He said I wouldn't owe him, but I just want to make my own way."

"Your brother must have a great job."

Kelly nodded. "He started a new job about three months ago. Not exactly sure what it is—I think he mentioned he's some kinda recruiter, but anyway."

"Maybe I should become a recruiter," I said.

"No kidding. He seems to make good money, but I think the job may be stressing him out."

"What makes you say that?"

"I don't know," she said with a shrug. "He's just always on edge."

I nodded.

"But anyway, whatta 'bout you?"

"Me? I'm just here looking at shoes."

Kelly smiled. "Anything you like?"

"Those boots over there caught my eye, but I'm not ready to get 'em just yet."

A group of young women entered the store.

"Well, you have customers to tend to," I said.

"Yeah…"

"Are you working at the diner tonight?"

"Yep. I'll be there."

"Okay. I might stop by to trouble you for some more grilled chicken."

Kelly smiled. I smiled back and walked toward the entrance.

"Bye, Anthony."

I paused, turned, and waved bye before exiting the store.

Small world.

CHAPTER
SIX

IT TOOK ME thirty minutes to walk back to the motel. The area was still very much empty except for a few parked cars and a couple of occupants standing outside their rooms. I walked to my door, and as I removed my key, I saw a silver streak from the corner of my eye. Vargas whipped the Focus into a parking spot a few spaces from my room.

I placed the key back in my pocket and walked to the passenger side. As I approached, he buzzed down the window.

"Good morning," Vargas said with a smile.

"Morning. You already have something lined up for me?" I asked.

Vargas shook his head. "Not yet, but soon. Hop in. Let's go for a ride."

"To where?"

Vargas hunched his shoulders. "Just somewhere we can talk over a cup of coffee."

I shrugged. "Okay," I said, while opening the door and sliding into the front passenger seat.

Vargas backed from the parking spot, sped toward the road, then made a right turn.

"You know there's a mall and shops back the other way?" I said.

Vargas nodded. "Yeah, but it can also get crowded there," he said. "I want to get some fresh air, but at a location where we don't have to be overly concerned about our cover IDs. You never know who you'll run into in busy areas. Know what I mean?" he said with a smile.

"That's true," I said. I knew exactly what he meant and considered telling him about my run-in with Long and his sister but kept it to myself. There were still a lot of unanswered questions I had about the operation, and I wanted to gather more details before I shared.

"So, what did you do with the rest of your night?" he asked, glancing at me before staring back at the road.

I looked out my window and watched as power lines and trees rolled by, raised the window to block the breeze from my eyes, then answered, "Had dinner, then went to bed."

"Where did you eat?"

"At a diner, across the street from one of the drop sites."

"Oh, speakin' of which," Vargas said as he looked at my side of the windshield and pointed. "There's another site up here."

I followed his finger and saw a gas station coming up. Before the station sat a parking lot with cracked pavement and concrete debris from what remained of a building. Near the road was a faded mailbox, just as I saw in the opposite direction.

"I see it. Thanks," I said.

"Of course, man." Vargas smiled again.

"Somebody's chipper. So, what'd you do last night?"

"I spent some time with my wife and kids."

"You have a son and daughter, right?"

Vargas glanced at me. "Yeah," he said while squinting.

"I saw the picture on your desk."

"Oh, okay."

"It's good you had the opportunity to see them. I know you mentioned you don't see them often enough—that has to be tough."

Vargas sighed. "It can be challenging, but I try to cherish every moment I have with them. They're my everything." He narrowed his sights on the road and his jaw muscle tensed. "I'll do anything to protect them."

I said nothing.

The rest of the drive comprised of Vargas making four turns, veering into a shopping plaza, and parking near a health food store. It took all of eight minutes, then another minute to walk across the sparsely occupied parking lot and enter the cafe. The inside was just as scantly occupied as the parking lot, with only two other customers besides me and Vargas. There was no one in line, so Vargas quickly ordered his latte, and I ordered a bottled water, then we sat at a table outside. The sun shined on my face and the wind breezed over me as I opened my water and took a gulp. Vargas lifted his cup and sipped, then placed the cup on the table and smiled. I just looked at him and listened as the birds squawked and traffic zoomed past on a nearby street.

"What?" he asked me.

I shrugged and shook my head.

"I'm happy we're finally making some headway on this case," Vargas said.

"I know you've been undercover for two months now, but how long have you been working this case overall?" I asked.

Vargas looked to the sky and squinted. "It's been close to four months."

"Thought you'd have it cracked by now?"

Vargas hunched his shoulders. "I don't know. Kinda. It took a couple months just to infiltrate and get my first fight. I'm ready to be done with this."

"That's understandable. Especially being a family man."

"So, what about you, Black?"

I said nothing.

"Who is Orlando Black?" Vargas continued.

"You know everything about me. It's all in that folder you guys have back at HQ," I said.

"Not everything. It doesn't say why a guy like you is passing through Texas."

"That's it. I was just passing through. I stopped for gas, saw someone I thought needed help, and, well—you know the rest."

Vargas stared at me as I took a swig of my water.

"Well, I'm happy you were passing through," he said, before sipping his coffee.

"That makes one of us."

Vargas chuckled, and as he did, his phone buzzed. He held a smile while placing the phone to his ear.

"Hi, Deidra," he answered before listening for a moment. "Yeah, I'm here with Black having a cup of coffee." He listened some more. "No, I haven't heard anything yet, and I will." The smile on Vargas' face dissolved as he listened once more. "Oh, um... Is something wrong? I left it all on your desk." He turned his face from me. "Yeah, I figured you could take it down to evidence. ... Okay, I'll let you know. Talk with you later."

Vargas stuffed his phone back inside his pocket, then looked at me.

"Is everything okay?" I asked.

He shrugged. "Yeah, just some administrative stuff."

I said nothing. Just watched as Vargas continued to drink his coffee.

We sat for another sixteen minutes and talked about how slick of a car I had before heading back inside the cafe. On the way out, I ordered a sandwich and a cup of fruit for later. The drive back was mostly quiet. Vargas appeared to be deep in his thoughts; I know I was. Contemplating if I should leave, make an excuse to go to HQ, lift my keys off Deidra, and drive off into the sunset with my slick car. But although Deidra seemed to operate somewhat off the books, I still would risk having law enforcement come after me. Especially now that the team felt I could help them close this case. And if I was honest with myself, there was something about the case that intrigued me. I'm not sure if it was the thrill of the matches, or the opportunity to take down some unsavory characters, or the feeling of satisfaction I received when I uncovered everyone's secrets, because there were some secrets and ulterior motives.

I looked at Vargas, and he took his eyes off the road to glance at me with a smile.

I forced a smile back at him. *That I'm sure of.*

When we arrived at the motel, Vargas parked directly in front of my room.

"Imma head back to the office. Hafta' check on some stuff," he said as I reached to open the car door. "But keep your phone handy—after your performance yesterday, I'm sure I'll get a call soon."

I nodded. "Copy that," I said before exiting the car and entering my room.

As the door closed behind me, I heard the Focus reverse from the parking spot, then cruise away. I locked the door, then tossed the bag with my sandwich and fruit cup on the bed before making my way to the bathroom. After using the toilet, I washed my hands, then sat on the bed and clicked on the television. Every station was either a news channel with a sensational headline, a soap opera, or a shopping channel, so I turned the television off and focused on my lunch.

I finished my meal in twelve minutes and flushed it all down with the water I had left in my bottle. Relaxing into my thoughts, I lay back on the bed with my hands cuffed behind my head. Regretting stopping at the gas station, regretting not leaving town immediately after I felt something was off, and wondering why I often found myself in situations that challenged my patience. I then realized that it had been a while since I had one of my episodes of rage. *I must really have it under control, because these past six months have really tried my patience.* A smile crossed my face as I realized something else; although people and their mess got on my nerves, a part of me enjoyed the excitement of danger, confrontation, the adventure of the unknown, and helping.

Before I could sink deeper into my thoughts, my phone vibrated. I rocked forward, removed the phone from my pocket, then flipped it open.

"Hello," I said into the phone.

"Hi, Black, it's Deidra."

"Good afternoon, Agent Harris."

"How's everything going? I talked to Vargas earlier. He said you two were having coffee."

"He had a cup of coffee. I had water."

"Oh, well, I assumed you were having coffee too. You know what I mean?"

"Not really. I don't like to assume—specifics matter."

"I didn't call to argue semantics."

"Not semantics. Specifics."

"Whatever. I called to see if you need anything."

"I'm fine."

"Okay—now it's important you have your phone with you at all times today. We're suspecting the show you put on yesterday is causing waves throughout the fight community. I'm sure the news has gotten back to the right people, and we'll be hearing something soon."

"Yeah."

"You're doing a good thing here, Black. You helped us secure fifty-thousand dollars of evidence."

"Fifty-thousand?" I said, expecting clarity.

"Yeah, fifty-thousand. The winnings from yesterday; Vargas left it all on my desk."

"Oh, right."

Deidra giggled. "Are you okay?"

"I'm good."

"Alright, let me know if you need anything. I have to go—stay by your phone."

"Got it," I said before ending the call.

Specifics matter, I thought before lying back and closing my eyes.

I opened my eyes two hours later and sat up in the bed before checking my phone. There were no missed calls or messages. I plugged the phone into the charger and walked to the bathroom. After washing my face, I walked back into the living area and found my phone ringing.

"White, It's Hector," Vargas said. "I have something for you. Interested?"

"Always."

"Good. I'll be there to pick you up in about an hour."

"I'll be here."

I ended the call and went to connect the phone back to the charger, but it vibrated in my hand.

"Hello," I answered, for the second time in the past three minutes.

"Hi, Black," Deidra said. "I got a call from Vargas. He—"

"Yeah, I talked with him. He's on his way."

"Okay, be careful, and keep me in the loop."

"Right," I said before again ending the call for the last time, I hoped.

I lay on the bed with my thoughts for thirty minutes, then stood and stretched before deciding to get some fresh air. The sun struck my eyes as I stepped outside. The temperature felt warm but comfortable. I stood at my door and watched as a dusty breeze swept across the parking lot. After taking three deep breaths, I strolled to the opposite end of the building. There was no one else around. The area was empty, dull, and frankly, boring. I liked it. It was a great place to think in solitude. I stood at the corner of the motel, staring at the sign for the diner while thinking about the case. Wondering about Deidra's motives, Vargas' motives, the mysterious man behind the question mark, and who I'd have to fight next. After staying that way for ten minutes, I pivoted toward my room, and as I took a step, I saw Vargas coasting into the parking lot.

He angled the Focus with the passenger side facing me.

"You're early," I said upon entering the car.

"We have a long drive," he said.

I shrugged, then pulled the seatbelt across my upper body as Vargas cruised out of the parking lot and veered onto the road. Vargas focused on the highway and appeared to be deep in his thoughts. We drove for twenty minutes without speaking, taking I-35 South most of the ride up to that point.

"So, we're heading south," I said.

Vargas glanced at me. "Yeah. Um… far south."

"To where exactly?"

He glanced at me again. "Let's just say we have another two hours of driving ahead of us." Vargas inhaled, then released a sharp exhale.

I felt my eyebrows furrow. "Are you okay?" I asked.

He looked at me through squinted eyes. "Yeah. Just have a lot on my mind," he said with a chuckle.

"I see."

"Hey, have you talked to Deidra today?"

"Yep."

"When?"

"Right after you dropped me off."

"Well… did she say anything?"

"Of course."

"What?"

"She said she had talked to you earlier and was checking to see if I needed anything."

"Okay," Vargas said, nodding at the wheel.

I eyed him. "Oh yeah. I had to clarify something for her."

Vargas whipped his head in my direction. His eyes widened and his breathing became heavier. "What? What was it?"

I smiled. "It was nothing."

"Whattaya mean?" Vargas asked, while sharing his gaze between me and the windshield.

I shrugged. "I don't think it was anything important."

"Well, tell me then."

"I told her I had water."

Vargas winced. "What?"

"She thought we both had coffee. I told her you had coffee, and I had water."

A crooked smile arched on Vargas' face. "Oh," he said with a slight chuckle. "I thought it was something about the case." He shook his head and fixed his eyes on the road.

I smirked. *All the signs of a man hiding something.*

CHAPTER
SEVEN

WE DROVE FOR another hour and forty-five minutes before arriving in Laredo. As we passed through the town, small buildings flanked us on both sides while pedestrians walked along the sidewalks and crossed by at every stoplight.

"Don't tell me we're going to Mexico, because I'm pretty sure that's out of your jurisdiction," I said.

Vargas smiled. "Nah. But don't worry, we're not too far away now."

I shrugged, then relaxed into my seat and watched as the buildings rolled by until trees, homes, and power lines replaced them. The smooth paved road soon became a bumpy dirt path and a rotten stench seeped into the car. I crinkled my nose and Vargas noticed.

"I know," he said. "There's a canal nearby full of sewage and animal carcasses. Another couple of miles and we'll be away from it."

I threw a nod at Vargas, then pinched my nose and did my best to limit my inhales. We continued up the road and across a bridge, then drove another five minutes before the smell disappeared. I rolled down my window and Vargas did the same. Fresh air breezed through the Focus as he leaned into a right turn. We bumped down the road for a mile, passing a few sparsely scattered houses and trees on either side. After driving another half of a mile, the houses and trees were nowhere to be found. Only dirt, rocks, and small hoodoos were present.

I looked at Vargas.

He glanced at me, smiled, then hunched his shoulders before placing his eyes back on the road. "They have these fights in some unusual places," he said. "It's about discreetness for them." He pointed at the windshield. "But we're almost there."

I followed his finger and saw a pair of rocky hills up ahead. The hills were about two-stories high with slight variations in texture and size, and a small opening separated the two structures. As we continued up the road, the base of the hills rolled into sight and at the bottom, a herd of vehicles sat parked in the grass and dirt. One hundred yards away from the vehicles, closer to us, two large SUVs were on either side of the road. Both vehicles sat perpendicular to the road with a man's silhouette standing in front of each. As we approached, the figures slowly revealed more details. The man on the left had dark espresso skin, a short, boxed-afro, a clean shave, and a sour look. His partner on the opposite side sported a bald head and a dark goatee stood out from his tan complexion. Both men had bulky muscles and wore a black suit and tie, as well as a Heckler & Koch MP5 draped from their shoulder.

I looked at Vargas. "I thought your boy Juan and his partner stood guard at the entrance."

Vargas stared at the windshield and gently shook his head. "There's some high-profile matches taking place here tonight, and—"

"High-profile matches mean high-profile recruiters, which means better security."

Vargas smiled. "Exactly. It also means we're closer to finding out who's supplying these cartels with drugs and money. I can't believe it. Feels like we've made more progress these past two days than in the last two months."

I said nothing, and faced the windshield as we approached the SUVs.

The guy with the boxed-afro stuck his palm out and Vargas slowed the Focus to a stop. The man gestured for Vargas to lower the window, then gripped his MP5 and walked toward the driver's side. Vargas buzzed down his window, and the man stared at him before glancing around the car's interior, then fixing on me. By that time, his bald partner made it to my side of the car and peeked through the back window.

"We're here for a match," Vargas said.

The man with the afro looked at him with a sour face. The look appeared to be his default disposition. Vargas winced as the man continued to stare at him.

Sour-face reached into his pocket and removed a cell phone. "Your name?" he asked Vargas.

"Hector. Hector Corrales," Vargas said.

The man swiped his thumb across the phone, and the guy on my side, the one with the bald head and goatee, walked to the front of the car, faced the windshield, then cradled his rifle.

The guy with the dark skin and sour face looked up from his phone and briefly glanced at me. "And his name?" he asked Vargas before looking back at his phone.

"Anthony White. He's a fighter."

The man craned toward the window and stared at me again, his eyebrows raised. "The Ghost?"

Vargas squinted, then nodded. "Yeah—yeah, he goes by Ghost," he said with a grin.

The man smirked. "I thought you'd be a little bigger."

I shrugged.

"Anyway," the man said as he stood straight. "We've been

expecting you." He flicked a hand gesture to his partner, then waved Vargas through.

The bald guy stepped off the road, and Vargas pulled forward and past the SUVs. From my side-view mirror, I saw the two men walking toward their respective vehicles.

"That's good," Vargas said.

I looked at him.

"It's good they're expecting you, is what I mean."

I sighed. "Maybe," I said.

We drove for another minute before Vargas veered the Focus off the road, through the dirt, and parked on the grass next to a white Bentley and a dark blue Jaguar. We exited the car and threaded through the field of vehicles toward the hills. The sun descended, casting a dim glow behind the tall, natural structures as we followed a small line of people between the cliffs. The space between the two hills was twenty feet wide, and two men in black suits armed with MP5s stood on either side of the entrance.

"Great. Two more," I uttered to myself.

Light beamed from the opening and soft techno music, along with the scents of cigars and alcohol, accompanied it. The men at the entrance stopped everybody one by one, had a brief exchange with each individual, then thumbed through their own phone before waving the person inside. When we were near the entrance, the guy on the left stuck his palm out toward us.

"Hold it," he said.

Vargas stopped first, and I stopped behind him.

"Your name?" the man asked.

Vargas moved his lips, then paused before saying, "Hector Corrales."

The man squinted and swiped at his phone. After a few seconds, he looked up. "Okay, so you're Hector Corrales," he said, before leaning to the side and peering around Vargas.

"And you must be…" he said to me while glancing down at the phone.

"Anthony White," Vargas said.

The man smiled. "Yeah-yeah, Anthony White. The Ghost."

I shrugged.

The man nodded while maintaining a crooked smile. "Heard a lot about you. C'mon in."

As we walked toward the entrance, Vargas leaned toward me.

"You're quite the celebrity here," he said.

I scoffed. "Popular within an organized crime community. Lucky me."

We followed a familiar looking short man inside. He wore a gray suit, his salt-and-pepper hair in a ponytail, and had a woman on each arm. Tall, jagged stony walls enclosed us, and short lamp posts lit the ground as we strolled along the passageway. With each step, the music grew louder and the cigar and alcohol scents strengthened. A slight chill of anticipation shot through my body, and as the chatter from random voices increased, so did my curiosity to see what waited ahead.

Seconds later, we stepped onto a grass field surrounded by rock dunes and towering cliffs. Generator powered flood lights, portable stadium lights, and LED bulbs inside the walls, illuminated the area. There were crowds of people scattered throughout, and at the center of the field was a square boxing ring. Strobe lights placed at all four corners brightened the empty platform with a white glow. Beyond the ring, on the opposite side, sat a booth with two windows.

Vargas said something I could barely make out.

I shrugged and shook my head.

He stepped closer. "We hafta' get you checked in," he said over the music and chitchat.

He then browsed the area. I did the same. To my left, I saw the short man we followed inside walk to a bar with the two ladies. He said something to the bartender, who nodded before turning to the shelf and grabbing a couple of bottles.

"There," Vargas said while pointing at the booth with the two windows.

I followed his finger, then him. We weaved around a few people before circling the ring and walking toward the booth. I glanced to my left and saw the short guy standing and the two ladies sitting at the bar, but they weren't alone. The short man was talking with two guys I'd seen before. Long and Snyder. Both men wore black suits with white shirts and no tie. The short man placed a hand on the back of each woman, said something to them, then trailed Long and Snyder. The three men disappeared behind a wall to the right of the bar. It piqued my curiosity, but I didn't give it too much thought. The fight and my opponent occupied my mind.

As we approached the booth, a woman on the opposite side stepped to the window. The tight, black dress she wore accentuated her curvy figure, and her pale skin brought out the color of her straight, dark brown hair and red lipstick.

She smiled. "How can I help you, gentlemen?" she said in a soft, slow tone.

Vargas returned the smile. "I—ah—we," he struggled for words.

The woman tilted her head, pursed her lips, and raised an eyebrow all in unison.

Vargas sighed and chuckled. "I'm sorry. We need to check in."

"As fighters?"

"Yes. Well, he's the fighter," Vargas said while pointing at me.

The woman looked at me through the thick glass, parted her lips, and slowly traced her eyes down to my legs, then back to my face.

"Your name?" she asked while lifting a computer tablet and pressing on the screen.

"My name is Hector Corrales," Vargas said.

"Not your name, his?"

"Anthony White," I said.

She smiled, then flicked at the tablet's screen. "Okay, Mr. White. You're in the main event, and it's in forty-five minutes."

Vargas glanced at me with squinted eyes. "Who's he fighting?" he asked her.

She stared at the screen. "Uhh... it looks like Jax."

Vargas' eyes widened. "Are you sure?"

"Yep. Will you be putting something on the fight?"

Vargas stared at the ground but didn't answer.

"Sir?" the woman said.

"Sorry," he said. "What was that?"

"Are you placing a bet?"

"Yeah, after I get my fighter situated."

"Alright, just make sure it's in before the fight starts."

"Got it. Where do we get ready?"

"Oh, yeah," she said, reaching under the counter. "There's a passageway to your right. Follow it until you reach the portables," she continued while sliding a ticket and a key under the window.

Vargas grabbed them.

"The ticket will get you access and the key is for your locker. It's inside the modular home with the flagpole. Make sure you wear the clothes inside the locker."

"Okay thanks," Vargas said.

As we turned away from the window, the women smiled and winked at me. I smiled back. We walked toward the passageway, and I noticed Vargas hanging his head.

"You okay?" I asked.

He looked up. "Yeah... yeah, let's get to the locker room."

As we walked through the passageway, I turned to him. "Is there something you want to tell me about this fighter, Jax?" I asked.

Vargas sighed. "He's a dangerous fighter, Black."

"Didn't you say the same thing about the other guy I fought?"

"I said he was one of the best fighters in the circuit."

I shrugged.

"But this guy is better, and he's dangerous. He already killed two men in the ring."

"If he has a weakness, I'll find it."

"I don't doubt you, but Black, you have to be careful."

On the other side of the passageway were more construction lights and a dirt field with scattered blotches of grass. Three rectangular portable homes oriented in the shape of a U sat at the center of the field. The portable at the bottom of the U had a flagpole with a black flag with red stripes flapping in the wind near the front door. Two guards, armed with the same MP5s as the other guards carried, circled the field.

"That must be where the locker room is," Vargas said, pointing at the mobile home with the flagpole.

As we crossed the field, one guard approached, halting us with one hand while placing his other hand on the gun draped over his shoulder.

"We have a match," Vargas said.

"You have a ticket?" the guard asked.

While Vargas handed him the ticket, I watched as the other guard paused and looked in our direction. The guard closest to us inspected the ticket, then gave it back to Vargas before waving us toward the portable with the flag.

"You're Ghost?" the guard asked me.

I nodded.

He smiled. "Good luck with your fight."

"Thank you," Vargas said as we walked past the guard and to the mobile home.

The inside was empty and reeked of a chalky odor. Sheetrock with streaks of drywall compound surrounded us. We walked to the left and around a partition wall and found the locker area. At the far wall were two doors, both labeled *bathroom*. Vargas looked at the key, then threaded around a bench to a group of lockers.

"Looks like it's this one," he said, pointing at a worn locker.

I walked to him, and he handed me the key. A faded padlock hung from the locker's latch. I inserted the key and swung open the door to find some black trousers, a black tank top, black Adidas with white stripes, and a pair of black MMA gloves inside.

"I guess they want you in all black," Vargas said.

"You think?"

Vargas chuckled as he walked back toward the partition. "I'm gonna let you change. Be right back," he said.

I didn't look at him, just said okay and waved before removing the clothes from the locker. It took me five minutes to change into the new clothes and secure my old ones inside the locker. Everything fit comfortably, even the shoes, which made me wonder who it was that sized me up. I placed the locker key inside my trouser pocket, then stretched and shadowboxed, and before I knew it, fifteen minutes passed and I heard footsteps creaking across the floor.

Vargas peeped around the partition.

"Ready?" he asked.

"Yeah."

We walked back to the field and found the ring surrounded by the crowd, clapping and cheering. Hands touched me as Vargas and I made it closer to the ring. At the center of the ring was a referee, and outside of the ring, near the corner opposite to us, stood a beige-skinned, hairy-chested, muscular man, wearing red shorts, red MMA gloves, and sporting a mohawk. He was shadowboxing from an orthodox stance. The man threw a left jab, followed by a right jab, then concluded his combination with a right roundhouse kick intended for his opponent's midsection. I watched him perform this combination three times. Each time he showed a slight hesitation before executing his kick.

When we reached the ring, Vargas turned to me.

"That's him, Jax," he said.

"I figured," I said.

"Be careful and don't try to be a her—"

I chuckled. "Don't worry. I got him."

Vargas winced. "Really?"

"Yeah. This fight shouldn't take long."

Vargas stared at me with his eyes squinted.

The referee walked to our corner and craned toward us through the middle and top ropes.

"You ready, black?" he said while looking at me.

Both Vargas and I looked at him and paused.

"Black?" I said.

"You're wearing black, right?" the ref said.

"Yes, I'm ready."

"Okay, let's go," the man said before walking back toward the center of the ring.

Vargas and I glanced at one another and shrugged as I hopped on the platform, then ducked between the ropes and entered the ring.

I stood in my corner as the guy in the red shorts entered the ring and walked to the opposite corner. He glared at me. I glared back even harder. I felt a smile arch on my face, because I already knew how this fight would end.

CHAPTER
EIGHT

WHAT I DIDN'T know was three hours later, I'd be standing in my motel room with a bag of food in hand and a gun aimed at me. It was a small, silver, stainless steel 9mm Ruger. I recognized the man holding the gun but hoped he didn't recognize me. It was Kody Snyder.

"Shut the door," he said.

"Who are you?" I said, pretending not to know him.

"Who I am doesn't matter. Just know I know who you are."

I took a step toward Snyder, and he stepped back.

"Well, if you knew who I was, you'd know I'm the last man you'd want to point a gun at unless you plan on using it."

"What'd you say?"

"Enough, Mr. Snyder," said a voice with a Hispanic accent coming from near my room's desk.

I peeked around Snyder and saw the short man with the ponytail sitting in the chair at the desk.

"Lower your gun," he told Snyder.

"I don't work for you."

"That may be true, but if your employer finds out you killed the talent—that won't end well for you."

"I'd do what he says," I told Snyder.

Snyder glared at me and gritted his teeth before lowering his gun. He squinted while staring at my face. "You know what? I think I've seen you somewhere," he said.

"Of course, you have. He was at the fight tonight, you idiot," Ponytail said.

"No, no, no. I've seen him before that."

I scoffed.

"Have you ever seen him before, Mr. White?" the short man asked me.

I shook my head, then stepped close to Snyder. "If I'd seen him before, he's so ugly, I'd want to forget."

Snyder's eyes narrowed and his jaw muscles tensed.

The short guy with the ponytail laughed. "Okay, you two relax," he said. "We have business to discuss."

"Who are you, and whatta ya want?"

He stood from the chair. "I'm what you'll call a... talent scout," he said.

I walked past him and placed my food on the desk. The aroma from the grilled chicken and steamed broccoli wafted from the bag.

"Smells good. What is it?"

"Dinner," I said.

He nodded. "You put on quite the performance tonight. And from what I heard, the other night too."

I shrugged.

The short man rubbed his hands together. "So, Mr. White, or the Ghost, as they call you, I want you to fight for me."

"I don't know about that."

"I'll make it worth your while."

"Why would I fight for a man whose name I don't know?" I said as I removed my Styrofoam container of food from the bag and set it on the desk. "And how did you know I was staying here?"

"I go by a few names, but you can call me Javier, Javier Ramos."

Ramos. That's where I saw you.

"And your friend was kind enough to tell us where you were staying."

"I don't have any friends."

"Mr. Corrales. You don't consider him your friend?"

"I met him a couple of nights ago in a bar," I said before sitting at the desk. "That doesn't qualify as a friendship."

Ramos raised a brow and poked his lip. "Well, your... manager, I guess. He told us where you were staying."

"You want me to fight for you, so why would he tell you where I'm staying?"

"I can be persuasive. Plus, you don't want him managing you."

"Yeah," Snyder said. "Everyone knows Hector's a loser."

I turned to my food, and as I did, the sound of tires crunching over gravel struck my ear. Snyder walked to the window, moved the curtain back a slit and peeked outside.

"Who is it?" Ramos asked.

"Looks like Ethan."

I removed my plastic silverware from the bag and began cutting my chicken. It was tender and juicy. Easy to cut through.

"So, Mr. White," Ramos said, turning toward me. "How about you let me manage you?"

"Why?" I asked before sticking a fork full of chicken and rice into my mouth.

"As I mentioned, I'll make it worth your while."

I shook my head and continued eating, figuring I better fill up while I could. Ramos just stared at me, then sighed. A second after that, three knocks came from the door. Snyder opened it, and Long walked inside before shutting the door behind himself and staring at me. I stared back and continued to chew my food.

"So, what are we doin'?" he asked.

"Mr. White was just about to take me up on my offer," Ramos said.

I glanced at him. "I'll have to talk to my current manager first," I said, before placing my attention back on my meal.

"I don't think you understand, Mr. White, your *previous* manager is out of commission."

Oh boy. That doesn't sound good for Vargas.

I played it cool and shrugged. "What do you mean?" I asked before forking some broccoli into my mouth.

"You're in need of a new manager. I mean, only a few people can take you to the next level, and I'm one of them."

"You said it paid well?" I said between chews.

"Very."

I nodded. "Okay, let me think about it."

Ramos sighed. "It's a lot of money. What's there to think about?"

"We don't have time to waste," Snyder said.

Ramos turned and pointed his palm at him, then faced me again. "Mr. White, we're on a tight deadline and need to know your answer right now. My friends here have to go back to their boss and get everything organized."

"Well then, I guess my answer is no," I said.

Ramos' eyes widened, and Snyder moved his gun from his side to the front of his chest.

"I'm afraid you may not have much of a choice," Ramos said.

I looked at him. "Oh, there's always a choice," I said before wiping the crumbs from my mouth and standing. "How much money are we talking about?"

"Your cut? A couple of hundred thousand, give or take."

I cuffed my chin, as if I was reconsidering the offer.

"And that's for only one fight," Ramos continued.

I nodded. "I tell you what, give me half the money up front now, then the rest after I win the fight."

Ramos scoffed.

"This guy can't be serious," Snyder said.

"Really confident," Long blurted.

"Let's say I paid you upfront, and you lose. How—" Ramos started.

"I won't lose. But to make you feel better, I'll give you half of what you pay me upfront back if that was to happen."

Ramos laughed. "The coconuts on this guy. You think I'm gonna pay you if you lose?"

"You think I'll fight for free?"

"How much did Hector pay you?"

"Doesn't matter. He's no longer my manager, remember? This is a different circuit, so different set of rules."

Now Ramos cuffed his chin as if he was considering my offer.

"Okay," he said while extending his hand. "Deal."

We shook on it.

"When we get to my compound, I'll get you your money."

"Naw. I'm sure you placed a bet on me tonight. And I'm pretty sure you made a lot off me."

"How do you know that?"

"Because you're willing to bet on me again. I'll be here waiting while you run to your car and get my hundred thousand."

Ramos looked over his shoulder. "Mr. Long, do you mind bringing in my briefcase from the car?"

Long nodded, then opened the door.

"Are you serious?" Snyder said.

"My fighter, my choice."

A few minutes later, Long entered the room with the brief-case in hand. He passed it to Ramos and Ramos thanked him before placing it on the bed and opening it. Multiple stacks of hundreds filled the case. A band wrapped each stack to identify it as ten thousand dollars. Ramos took ten stacks from the briefcase and tossed them on the bed.

"Now, do we have a deal?" he asked.

I picked up one stack and inspected it. I ran my thumb across the edge of the bills, causing each bill to fan. They were crisp and carried that strong, paper and metallic scent new bills have.

"Yeah, we have a deal," I said with a crooked smile, pretending the money completely motivated me.

From the corner of my eye, I saw Ramos smile.

"Good," he said. "We should be on our way, then. There's much to discuss."

"Absolutely, but first if you gents don't mind," I said, nodding at the money on the bed.

"Of course," Ramos said before closing the briefcase, turning to Snyder and Long, then pointing to the door.

Long immediately opened the door, and Snyder rolled his eyes. Four seconds later, all three men went outside. I went to the dresser and removed a pair of jeans, a couple of shirts and boxers, a sweatshirt, and a pair of sweatpants. I put eighty thousand into the pockets of the spare jeans, and the remaining twenty thousand I stuffed into the pockets of the jeans I was wearing. From the desk, I removed the bag for my food and placed all the clothes inside it. When I stepped outside, the three men stood by the Cayenne, chatting.

"Are you ready, Mr. White?" Ramos asked.

"Yeah," I said before locking and shutting the door behind myself. While observing the doorknob and locking mechanism, a thought crossed my mind. "Did you guys return my room key?"

Ramos shook his head. "No. We had a… talk with the guy at the front desk. He doesn't mind if we hold on to it for a little while."

"Right."

We entered the SUV. Long sat behind the wheel with

Ramos in the front next to him, and I sat behind Ramos in the back seat with Snyder to my left. Long flicked on the head-lights, put the vehicle in gear, and ten seconds later we were on the road. We drove for an hour, mostly in silence, mostly southwest.

"So, where's this compound of yours?" I asked Ramos.

He glanced around his headrest and smirked. "Try to get some sleep, Mr. White. We have a long couple of days ahead of us," he said before turning and relaxing into his seat.

I shrugged and caught Snyder looking at me. I stared back for a moment before cutting my eyes and relaxing into my seat, figuring I'd take Ramos' advice and get some rest. The Cayenne's dashboard clock showed 12:42 a.m. I made a note, closed my eyes, and drifted into a light sleep, but remained aware of my surroundings. I opened my eyes to the SUV easing to a stop. Both Ramos and Snyder were asleep, and Long was buzzing down his window. The clock showed 1:38 a.m. As a border patrol officer approached the vehicle, I looked up and saw a large sign welcoming us to Mexico. The man flashed his light inside and winced as if he recognized Long.

"You're good," the man said as he waved Long through.

We crossed the border and Long drove a hundred yards from the checkpoint before pulling off the road. He exited the car, then knocked on Snyder's window. Snyder jumped out of his sleep, rubbed his hand across his face, then through his short brown hair before turning to his window and sighing.

"Your turn to drive," came Long's muffled voice from the other side of the window.

Snyder stretched, then opened his door. The two men danced around each other, and a few seconds later Snyder was at the wheel and Long was in the backseat with me. A moment after that, the SUV eased back onto the road and I closed my eyes enough to rest them, but not so much to where I couldn't track where we were going. After two more hours of driving, we ended up on the outskirt of Nuevo Leon, near the mountains. Snyder veered onto a back road, and we drove for a half of a mile before the vehicle's headlights beamed on a large, enclosed area. The wall was a light shade of orange with white trim. At the front entrance, a guard stood outside a security hut. He immediately walked inside the hut as if he recognized the vehicle, then a moment later, the steel gate slid open. On the other side, post lights lit a large yard with lush, green grass and manicured hedges. Thirty yards up the driveway was a two-story house that shared the same color as the outside wall. As we approached the house, I noticed two more guards, one at each end of the front of the house. The driveway circled at the front of the house, and at the center of the circle was a marble statue of a man with a sword in his hand. On the other side of the yard, to my right, was a one-story house with the same orange and white colors.

Ramos groaned. "Oh, we're here," he said.

"Yep," Snyder said with a sigh.

We circled the driveway and Snyder stopped the SUV at the front door. As we exited the vehicle, the guard from the east corner of the house walked to us. He was tall and had a FX-05 Xiuhcoatl draped over his shoulder.

"Welcome back, sir," he said to Ramos. "Do you need me to get anything?"

Ramos shook his head. "No." He then looked at Long and Snyder. "I do hope you two plan on staying until daylight. I have more than enough room."

The two men looked at each other and nodded.

"Okay then, let's get you to your rooms."

The front door opened, and a chubby little girl ran outside. "Daddy, you're home," she said, running into Ramos' arms.

He picked her up and embraced her. "What are you doing up?"

"Waiting on you."

"Oh, Dios mío," came a voice from the door.

A fit woman in a robe with deep tan skin and long, straight black hair jogged outside and toward Ramos. Long and Snyder stared at her as she grabbed the little girl and gave Ramos a kiss on the check. "Let's go back inside—Daddy's busy."

"I'll be in shortly," Ramos said, waving at the girl.

The woman and the girl went inside.

Of course you'd have a family.

Ramos shared his gaze between me, Long, and Snyder.

"Okay, gentlemen," he said. "We've had a long night, so let's get some rest and talk business over breakfast in the morning." He turned to the security guard. "Show them to their rooms."

"Sí señor," the guard said before pointing to the guesthouse.

Snyder walked in that direction, and Long followed him. I gripped my bag of clothes and followed the two men at a distance while the guard trailed behind me. I glanced over my shoulder and saw Ramos enter the main house.

When we reached the guesthouse, another guard met us at the front door. He was tall and had a mean look on his face.

"We need to show them to their rooms," the first guard told him.

The tall man nodded, then stepped to the door. When he unlocked and opened it, the first guard made his way back toward the main house.

"In here," the tall guard said while waving us inside.

We walked into a foyer where the guard flicked on a switch and light chased out the darkness. The foyer opened into a living room, and beyond the living space was a kitchen. To the right was a long hall, and to the left, a shorter hall, and at the opposite end of the house was a back door.

"You two, follow me," the guard said to Long and Snyder.

They followed him down the long hall. Fifteen seconds later, I heard a door open, followed by some talking. Moments after that, I heard more talking, followed by a door shutting. I scanned the interior for another thirty seconds before the guard returned.

He gestured for me to follow him. "Your room's over here," he said, walking past me and toward the short hallway.

The hallway contained three doors. One on either side of the hall, and one at the end of the hall.

"This is your bathroom," the guard said as we passed the first door to the left. "This is the gym," he said, pointing to the door on the right as we continued down the hall. "And this is your room," he finished when we stopped near the door at the end of the hall.

I thanked the guard, and he nodded, then turned and walked away. The inside of my room felt cooler than the hall. It had a king-size bed, a large rectangular window with blinds, a desk, dresser, and near the back of the room was a door. I walked across the hardwood floor and tossed my bag on the bed before making my way to the door. I opened it to find a walk-in closet. Nothing on the clothing racks or shelves. It was completely empty. Once I left the closet, I scanned and searched the room for any bugs or monitoring devices but found nothing. Peeking through the window blinds, I could see the side of the main house. I saw the same two guards at the front, but also noticed a guard I'd never seen before emerging from the shadows near the back. As I stepped away from the window and did some math in my head, my phone rang.

"White, speaking," I answered.

CHAPTER
NINE

"OH, GOOD YOU'RE okay," Deidra said through the phone.

"Kinda," I said. "Where were you? Been trying to call."

"Got a call from Vargas—he sounded worried. We're out searching for him. Been calling him all night but it goes straight to voice mail—and what do you mean kinda? Is he with you?"

"No. After my match, he got in the car with Ramos, Long, and Snyder."

"What? Was he forced? Ramos who?"

"Said his name was Javier Ramos," I said before shrugging at the phone. "I'm not sure if Vargas was forced or not. Hard to tell."

"Javier. We know him. Where are you now?"

"Ramos' house."

"Really? Where at?"

"Mexico."

The line went silent.

"It's located outside of Nuevo Leon near the mountains," I continued.

"Black... I..."

"I know. It's a bit out of your jurisdiction. But like everyone keeps telling me, I really didn't have a choice."

"No—well—yeah, I mean, we'll find a way to get jurisdiction. I'm just trying to process everything. This operation's going south. I'm guessing Ramos wants you to fight for him?"

"Affirmative."

Deidra sighed. "Okay, let me think." The line went silent again. "Did they give any hints to Vargas' location?"

"They didn't."

"Oh, no."

"Let's not assume the worst just yet."

Deidra inhaled. "You're right," she said while exhaling. "But until we find out what happened to Vargas, your number one priority is to get information on his whereabouts. We've pinpointed the location of his cell phone, but still want you to do some digging from the inside, just in case."

"Of course."

"And your second priority is to gather more details about your location. Try to find an address or something. On our side, we'll be working with our contacts in Mexico to see if we can figure it out, too. Is there anything you can tell us about the house? Size, color, whatever you can think of."

"Sure."

"Wait, let me put you on speakerphone," she said as static briefly filled the line. "Okay, go."

"It's a two-story, light orange house with white trim. The guesthouse, where I'm staying, is east of the main house and is the same color. There's a circular driveway with a marble statue sitting in the center. Also, the compound is behind a wall and there's a security shack at the front gate."

"Armed guards?"

"Yeah. FX-05 Xiuhcoatl and side arms. Five guards outside, including the one at the front gate and possibly two more inside the main house."

"Wow. How long have you been there?"

"Just got here."

"Impressive. Anything else that can help?"

"Not right now."

"Okay. Did you get all of that, Jess?" Deidra said.

"Got it," Jessica's voice answered through the speaker.

More static filled the line.

"Thanks," Deidra said into the phone. "I'll call and check in with you a few times throughout tomorrow."

"About that. It'd be better if I call you. That way I can make sure I'm alone before calling."

"Good point, but we can text on the phone, too. So if there's an emergency, I'll text you. Just remember the texts auto-delete three minutes after you read them. And the password to enter the SMS section of the phone is the last four digits of my number."

"Got it. I better get some rest. I have a feeling things are gonna get interesting today."

"You should. We'll be up, working. Have to get on top of this operation."

I said nothing.

"Black, I'll be in touch. And please, be careful."

"Copy that."

I ended the call before emptying the contents of my pockets and adding the twenty thousand dollars with the other eighty in my bag. My next stop was the bathroom where I washed up before returning to the main room, plugging my phone into the charger, and turning in for the night. While lying in bed, I thought about Vargas and if he was okay. I did this for two minutes before following the same advice I gave Deidra about not assuming the worst. There were many unanswered questions, and me being tired wouldn't help the situation, so I closed my eyes and drifted off.

. . .

I WOKE SIX hours later to sunlight seeping through the window blinds, and someone knocking on my bedroom door. I rolled out of bed and yawned as I made my way to answer it. On the other side stood the tall guard.

"The boss says breakfast will be in half an hour," he said with the same mean look he had the night before.

"I'll be there," I said before closing the door.

I made the bed, washed up, then threw on some clothes. It took me all of twenty minutes. Before leaving my room, I placed my bag of clothes with the one hundred thousand dollars inside in the bottom dresser drawer, under a fresh set of bed linens. I left the room and walked down the hall, past the foyer, and into the living room. As I searched the area for mail or anything that could give me an address of my location, I heard whispers coming from the kitchen's back door. I walked to the door and slowly lifted its window blind a slit. Long stood outside on a patio deck with his back to the door and his phone to his ear.

"I told you I'm fine, Kelly," he said into the phone. "No—no, I'm not stressed out. Look, I'll talk with you later," he finished before dropping the phone from his ear and turning toward the door.

I stepped away from the window and power-walked to the living room. The door opened, and he walked inside while shaking his head and exhaling.

"You okay?" I asked.

"Yeah, I'm good. You going to breakfast?" he said.

"Heading there now."

"Me too."

We left the guesthouse and made our way to the main house. The morning dew rolled off the grass, and the birds seemed to chirp with each step. As we approached the front, I saw Snyder standing near the door chatting with a security guard.

"There you are," he said to Long. "He's waiting for us in the backyard."

"Alright," Long said as he walked toward the door.

And as he did, Snyder eyed me. I eyed him back, then scoffed before following Long inside the house. A checkered marble floor, along with a grand staircase and a floral scent, greeted us in the foyer. Snyder said something to the guard outside as he entered behind us. A moment later, a butler appeared from behind the staircase and welcomed us. He ushered us from the foyer, past the staircase, through a sitting room and kitchen, and to a set of French doors. On the other side of the doors, was a long rectangular patio with another armed guard standing watch. We dodged around some patio furniture and walked alongside the pool for a few seconds before reaching a gazebo. Underneath it was a table with Ramos sitting at the head. He gestured for me to sit next to him, then thanked the butler for bringing us. I sat in the seat perpendicular to his right, while Long sat one chair down from me. Snyder circled the table to sit directly across from Long. Plates, cups, eggs, tortillas, salsa, mixed fruit, water, and coffee lay on the table. Long and Snyder began helping themselves to the food.

"Everybody dig in," Ramos said.

I placed a couple of tortillas and some eggs on my plate. I dressed them up with salsa on top and fruit on the side. As I filled my cup with water, I heard Ramos clear his throat.

"So, Mr. White," he said, "I figure we'll get right to your training after breakfast. Since the fight is tomorrow night and all."

I took a bite of my food and looked at him as the savory eggs, spicy salsa, and buttery tortilla bounced on my tongue and hit my taste buds.

"I'm confident you'll do well," he continued. "But the guy you're fighting can be a handful. That's why my trainer will be here in an hour so you two can run through some speed, strength, and endurance drills."

I continued to chew my food and look at him.

"I'm thinking you guys can train all day today, do some light training tomorrow morning, then you rest until the fight that night. What do you say?"

I swallowed my food. "Sure, whatever."

Ramos shrugged. "Okay, that's what we'll do then." He shared his gaze between Long and Snyder. "Mr. Snyder—Mr. Long. You can let your employer know my fighter will be ready tomorrow night."

Long and Snyder, both having a mouth full of food, nodded.

"Okay," Ramos said while hunching his shoulders. "After breakfast, we'll talk about my cut and that'll conclude our business. Buen provecho," he concluded before stacking his plate.

We sat and ate for another fifteen minutes before everyone's plate was clean. Snyder gulped down some water before wiping his mouth with the back of his hand and facing Ramos.

"Thanks for the hospitality and breakfast, but we should be going now," he said standing from the table.

Ramos also stood. "Of course, but we still have some business to discuss. We can go to my office," he said.

Long and I stood, and the four of us walked into the house. As we approached the foyer, I heard soft footsteps closing in on us from the hall. The same chubby little girl from the night before ran to Ramos and hugged his lower torso. Ramos arched down and hugged her back.

"Where's your mama?" he asked.

As he spoke more footsteps clacked against the floor, and a moment later, the same fit, deep tanned woman with long, straight, black hair appeared from the hall. She wore a tight black dress, and black heels with red bottoms. Long and

Snyder stared as the woman grabbed the little girl and led her toward the front door.

"We'll be out shopping," the woman said to Ramos.

"Absolutely, dear," Ramos said.

The front door opened and the butler stood on the other side. "The car's ready, señora," he said.

"Gracias," she said before waving to Ramos and guiding the little girl out the door.

"Adios, Papa," the girl said on her way out.

Ramos smiled. "Adios, baby," he said before turning to the rest of us. "Kids, they're wonderful."

Long and Snyder glanced at each other.

I said nothing.

"Thanks for breakfast," Snyder said while walking toward the door, with Long following him.

"One minute," Ramos said. "We still have to conclude our business," he continued while pointing down the hall.

Snyder rolled his eyes, then he and Long walked toward the hall. Ramos took a step after them but turned to me as if he forgot something.

"Mr. White—" he started.

"Let the trainer know I'll be in the gym warming up," I interrupted.

Ramos extended his index finger, then flicked his wrist. "Good. That's what I want to hear," he said with a smile.

The three men disappeared down the hall, and shortly after, I heard a door open, then shut. With my head on a swivel, I walked to the sitting room and browsed the coffee and end tables, hoping to find a document with an exact address, but had no such luck. I continued into the kitchen where I scanned the counter tops. *Nothing*. Noticing the kitchen island had sliding drawers, I reached for the handle of one. Just as my hand touched the handle, I heard a voice.

"Do you need help with something, sir?" the voice said.

I turned to find the butler standing behind me, with his

eyes squinted and his forehead wrinkled.

"Yeah, do you have a pen and pad?" I asked, with no hesitation.

"Oh," the butler said as his eyes widened and the wrinkles left his forehead. "It's here." He pulled open the drawer next to the one I had reached for and removed a thick pad with narrow white sheets of paper.

I grabbed the pad, then placed it on the island countertop while the butler removed a pen from his inner coat pocket and handed it to me.

"Thanks," I said as I wrote on the pad.

The butler stood and watched as I wrote a list of words such as stretching, cardio, sit-ups, push-ups, punching bag, etc. When I was done, I ripped the piece of paper from the pad, stuck it in my pocket, then handed him back his pen.

"Thank you," I said.

He placed the pen back inside his pocket while I brushed past him and walked toward the front door. After exiting the house, I immediately made my way to the guesthouse. I figured it should be empty and I could search around for clues to my location, but a security guard I hadn't seen before was sitting on the couch in the living room. He nodded, and I nodded back before making my way to my room. I lay on the bed with my thoughts for a few moments before deciding to keep up appearances by working out in the gym. It was a large room with treadmills, benches, weights, a refrigerator full of bottled waters, a punching bag, a couple of open areas with mirrors, and at the back was a sauna. I stretched, then started on the punching bag. After nearly fifty punches, the gym door opened and a tall, athletic guy with blue warm-up pants and a white tank top entered. He looked at me before scratching his receding hairline and combing his fingers through his slicked-back hair. After I glanced him over and saw he wasn't a threat, I continued punching the bag.

"Very good, very good," he said with a Spanish accent.

"You have great form."

I said nothing, just continued and added a couple of kicks to my punching combinations.

The man's eyes widened. "Nice. Your kicks have some serious power. I was a professional MMA fighter, so I know powerful attacks when I see them." He stepped closer to the punching bag. "I'm the trainer."

I stopped hitting the bag and looked at him. "Figured this much."

"I heard about your fight two nights ago, and I saw the one last night—and from what I see with the bag, your attacks and defense look solid. Where did you learn to fight?"

I shrugged. "Here and there," I said.

The trainer grinned. "Right. Since we don't have much time to train and you obviously know how to fight, I think it'll be best to focus on strength, speed, and your overall fighting endurance."

"Sure," I said.

"Let's get to it," he said, clapping his hands together.

We spent an hour lifting weights and going through foot-work drills. It was nothing big, nothing challenging or new to me. Nothing at all I felt would take my fighting to the next level, but I continued to play along.

"Let's take a break," the trainer said. "Your movements are accurate and fluid. Where did you say you train?"

I smiled. "I didn't."

He chuckled and smiled. "You're in good shape, but I want to keep your upper body hardened for the fight. Your opponent is—"

Before the trainer could finish his sentence, the gym door swung open and Ramos stepped inside with a guard. Ramos was slightly out of breath and had beads of sweat on his fore-head and darting eyes.

"Mr. White—I need you to come with me immediately," he said.

CHAPTER
TEN

THE TRAINER AND I looked at each other. I started to ask Ramos why, but figuring my question would soon be answered, I decided to just go along with it. Following him and the guard out of the guesthouse, we walked toward the main house where a silver limousine with dark, tinted windows sat parked in the front.

"New car?" I asked Ramos.

He didn't answer, just sighed and lowered his head, but when we arrived at the limousine, he turned to me.

"I'll no longer be your manager."

"What are you talking about?"

Ramos pointed at the limousine. "Your new manager is waiting for you, Mr. White."

I glanced at the limo, then looked at Ramos. Ramos hung his head, and the guard stepped to me.

"Please, sir," the guard said while pointing at the limousine's back passenger door.

I sighed and shook my head as I opened the door and slid into the vehicle. I immediately heard a voice over the car door slamming shut behind me.

"It's an honor to meet you, Mr. White," the voice said.

Across from me sat a man with dimples and dark, combed-back hair. I had seen him before. It was Christopher Navarro. He wore a slate blue suit and looked exactly like he did in the picture at the DEA headquarters. Sitting next to him in a dark gray suit was a slightly bulky man with an athletic build. He had a wide head, square chin, and a crooked nose.

"Who are you?" I asked Navarro, squinting as if I had never seen or heard of him before.

"My manners. I'm Chris Navarro," he said before nodding to the man in the gray suit. "And this gentleman to my side is Ivan."

"Okay. What's going on—what do you want?"

Navarro glanced over his shoulder while tapping his knuckle against the window behind him, and the limousine eased into gear and pulled off. Navarro flapped the collars of his blazer and adjusted in his seat.

"I have a proposition for you," he said.

"Yeah, and what's that?"

"I'd like you to fight for me."

I scoffed. "What is it with you guys? I've had two different managers in the past twenty-four hours, and now someone I don't even know wants me to fight for them."

"It'll be worth your while."

"That's the same thing Ramos said, and he's already paid me."

"Really? How much?"

I didn't answer.

"How does three hundred and fifteen thousand sound?"

I looked at Navarro as if I was interested.

He smiled. "I'm guessing Ramos isn't paying you that much."

I said nothing.

"Even if you lose, you get paid half of it."

"And what about Ramos?"

"I've already taken care of it. He won't be a problem."

"How?"

Navarro waved his palm at me. "Don't worry about it. The only thing I want you focused on is the fight tomorrow night."

"Okay," I said. "But I'll need my own space, and a place to train."

Navarro poked his lips and nodded. "Of course," he said before turning to the Ivan and holding his hand out. "But we have a few... interview questions, if you will."

Ivan grabbed a manila folder that lay in the seat next to him and handed it to Navarro before opening his blazer and placing his hand on the butt of a gun.

"So, where did you say you're from?" Navarro asked as he opened the folder.

"Connecticut," I answered with my eyes still on Ivan.

Navarro flipped through the documents in the folder. "You've been in trouble most of your life, even spent some time in the big pen. What for?"

I sighed and shook my head. "Armed robbery and attempted murder. It's all there in your folder, I'm sure, so why ask me?"

"You can never be too careful, Mr. White," Navarro said as he closed the folder. "Speaking of which, do you have any ID on you?"

I looked at him, then glanced at Ivan before slowly removing my wallet and handing Navarro the cover license Deidra gave me. He stared at the front for a moment then flipped it over and did the same on the back. After a minute, he handed it back to me.

"I'm still curious how a man like you became an underground fighter. And an outstanding fighter at that, probably the best I've ever seen."

I shrugged. "I wonder the same thing."

"How long have you known Hector Corrales?"

"Not long at all. Met him a few nights ago at a bar."

"Hmm."

"You know Corrales?" I asked.

"I know of him," Navarro said. "He seems like some lowlife wannabe."

Ivan laughed.

"But he sure got lucky with you," Navarro finished.

I shrugged. "If you say so."

Navarro smirked, then spent the next thirty minutes telling me how he thought I was one of the best fighters he has ever seen and bragging about the success and financial benefits of the fight organization. He had a smile on his face the entire time he explained. He seemed happy and proud. The car slowed before turning off the main road and onto a side street. Trees flanked us on either side as we snaked up the street and approached a tall wall. It was like the wall at Ramos' house except it was off white with black trim. The car stopped at a tall, black wrought iron gate and the driver said something before pulling forward. I looked to the driver's side window and saw two guards standing near a security hut, and when we had driven about fifteen yards, I glanced at the back window just in time to see the gate automatically close.

"Don't worry," Navarro said. "You're safe here."

I said nothing, just looked to the front of the car. We cruised along the smooth driveway for fifteen seconds before approaching a mansion, or castle maybe. The limousine circled and stopped at a flight of concrete steps. Two different guards opened the vehicle's passenger side door and I, Navarro, and Ivan exited, in that order. The steps rose twenty levels and at the top was a large wooden door. The mansion was the same off-white color as the outside walls surrounding it, and windows glared at us from all three stories. I glanced to my left, then to my right and saw a large yard with grass so green it looked like turf. The sweet, sharp smell of the lawn and flowers wafted by as we made our way up the steps.

When we reached the top, the front door opened, and a maid greeted us with a smile and behind her stood yet another guard.

"Welcome back, señor Navarro," the guard said to Navarro before looking at Ivan and nodding.

The maid and guard stepped back as Navarro and Ivan entered the house. I followed them, but the guard stuck his palm out and stopped me in my tracks. Navarro and Ivan turned and looked at me.

Navarro hunched his shoulders and shook his head. "I'm sorry. It's protocol," he said, watching the guard frisk me.

When the guard ran his hands across my pocket, I felt him pat his hand against my cell phone. He removed it from my pocket and handed it to me before continuing down my legs where he found my knife holsters. The guard removed both from around my ankles, then stood and raised them to Navarro.

Navarro stepped to the guard and removed one knife from its holster. "You can fight, so I'm guessing you're pretty good with this too, huh?" he said while waving the blade in the air.

I shrugged. "I guess I'm okay."

Ivan scoffed.

Navarro smirked. "I tell you what," he said as he placed the knife back inside the holster. "You can either keep your knives or your cell phone, but not both."

I looked at him, and he stared back at me.

A test, I thought before asking, "Really?"

"Really."

"Alright," I said, quickly tossing him the phone and taking my holsters from the guard.

As I knelt and strapped the holsters around my ankles, Navarro flipped the phone open and pressed at the keypad.

He fixed on the screen for a good ten seconds before glancing up at me.

"Whoa," he said. "Is Hector your only friend? You don't talk to anyone else?"

"Do I strike you as a man who likes to talk on the phone?"

Navarro chuckled and closed the phone. "No, you don't," he said, while tossing the phone back to me. "Come in. We have business to tend to."

I placed the phone inside my pocket, brushed past the guard, then followed Navarro and Ivan through the enormous foyer. There was a double staircase leading up to the other two floors. We walked between the stairs and made a right down a hall, and as we did, an older man limped from the hall and nearly collided into Ivan.

Ivan's eyebrows crinkled, and his nostrils flared. "Watch where you're going, old man," he said.

The man bowed his head, then quickly shuffled over until he was against the wall. His espresso skin shone under the glint of a strip of sunlight entering through from an upstairs window. He kept his head down and rubbed his hand across his forehead and through his salt-and-pepper afro. I locked eyes with him as we walked by. They were brown and familiar looking. The man's eyes moved from my eyes to my head. He stared with his mouth gaped and his eyes squinted. I squinted my own eyes and shook my head before turning my attention to the backs of Navarro and Ivan.

Interesting, I thought as I followed the two men into the hall. The hall was well lit, and we passed a few shut doors on either side before making it to a pair of double doors at the far end. Ivan opened one side of the door and held it while Navarro and I entered. The inside surprised me, and maybe even excited me a little. It was a large space filled with a boxing ring, a line of punching bags, weights, benches, treadmills, and an octagon cage at the far end. While I stood and listened to strikes echoing from a punching bag, Ivan walked past me and continued into the room.

Navarro looked at me. "You like?" he asked with a smirk on his face.

I nodded. "Yeah," I said as we walked side by side.

"Being the enthusiast I am, I had this gym added to the house. Cost me a little over a quarter of a million."

Yeah, of dirty money. The moment that thought left my mind, I felt my phone vibrate in my pocket. Navarro didn't appear to hear it, and I made no sudden movements. Just continued to stroll through the gym alongside him.

"This is all nice, but when am I gonna get paid?" I said.

"You get paid if you win."

"I'll win, so you can pay me half now, and the other half later."

"If you win, you get paid. If you don't—well, you get nothing."

Navarro pointed at a man attacking a punching bag. "That's pretty standard for all fighters," he continued.

"You said I get paid, win or lose, and I can count the number of guys training in here on one hand. Four guys is a far cry from all fighters," I said.

"Are you questioning me, Mr. White?"

I glanced at the ceiling sarcastically. "I guess I am."

Navarro stopped walking, and I did the same. He starred at me with his eyes narrowed and his jaw muscles tensed.

"That would be a mistake," he said.

I just looked at him. Didn't flinch. Didn't show any emotion.

"Plus, you're still being interviewed," he said as we continued to walk.

We approached Ivan, who was watching two men spar inside of the octagon cage. Both men were ripped and hard. One was short with a bald head, and the taller one wore his hair in a topknot.

"There's still the performance portion of your interview," Navarro said.

I looked at him but said nothing.

"Get in the cage," he said in a demanding tone.

"And if I don't?" I said.

Ivan stuck his hand inside his blazer, removed a pistol, and held it to his side.

"Mr. White, do you know what Ivan's holding?" Navarro said. "You're good with your fists and maybe even your little knives, but as you can see, we're not as primitive when it comes to our business."

I gave Ivan a mean stare, then shifted my scowl to Navarro as I made my way to the cage.

When I get my hands on you, I'll show you primitive. And it's a Sig Sauer P320 9mm with a 15-round magazine capacity, scumbag.

While I entered, the two men inside the cage turned to face me and Navarro gestured for Ivan to close the cage door.

Navarro stepped to the cage and gripped between the chain links with both hands. "Okay, gentlemen," he said. "We have a bit of a dilemma. There's one spot for the big fight tomorrow night, but three of you."

The man with the bald head squinted. "I didn't know we were being considered for that fight, boss," he said.

"You are now. All you have to do is beat Mr. White here—the Ghost." Navarro paused and rolled his eyes upward to the left as if he had a thought. "Let's make it interesting. Both of you versus him. If you win, one of you will be the contender in tomorrow night's fight."

The two men looked at one another and nodded. I glared at Navarro.

He shrugged. "What? It's business. I need to know I have the best fighter representing me."

I grinned at Navarro, and he winced at the sight.

Oh, when I get my hands on you, I thought before turning my attention from Navarro to the men in the cage with me.

The two men faced me and raised their gloved hands to a fighting position.

"Bare-knuckled," Navarro said as he stepped back from the cage.

The two men looked at each other once more, then removed their gloves, turned to me, and raised their fists again. I widened my stance and brought my fist to about chest height. We stayed this way for ten seconds before Navarro yelled, "Get on with it!"

The bald guy charged at me with a punch. I parried the attack with my right arm and used my left hand to push his shoulder. The cage rattled as he hit the mesh. His partner with the topknot launched a high roundhouse kick at me. I bobbed and a breeze rushed past the top of my head. He continued his attack with a sidekick. I stepped back and swatted the kick away. Out of the corner of my eye, I saw movement, then heard a grunt from that same direction. When I looked, Baldy soared toward me with a flying kick. I pivoted in time to dodge the kick and push him in the back. The force sent him crashing into the cage again, but much harder. He bounced off the mesh, then smacked onto the mat.

Seeing his partner on the ground and shaken up, Topknot growled and rushed me with two punches. I blocked both strikes. He caught me in the solar plexus with a kick, barely, but enough that I felt it. I stumbled back a step and glared at the man. Heat rose from my gut, and I felt the tension in my jaws as I gritted my teeth. I was mad, and it wasn't because of his insignificant kick. No, this was something more. I was tired of being everyone's pawn. Which was unfortunate for the two men in the cage with me.

Topknot leapt toward me with a flying punch. I jumped backward, spun one-hundred and eighty degrees in the air, and delivered a back kick to his gut. He dropped to his knees, then hugged his stomach before rolling to his side on the mat. Footsteps approached on my left. Baldy raced toward me with a wild right punch. As I ducked under the attack, he swung that same fist back around at me. I blocked his attacking arm and smashed my elbow into his right jaw before hip tossing him. He fell back first on the mat. I knelt to one knee and struck him in the face with a solid punch. His head jerked back, and he grunted before sprawling on the mat. When I stood, Topknot was crawling to his feet. While walking past him, I paused to knee him in the face and he fell back down.

Navarro clapped. "Well done, Mr. White. Well done," he said, making his way into the cage.

Ivan followed behind him.

"You're a great fighter, indeed," Navarro continued as he approached me. He placed his hand on my shoulder. "And you're going to win tomorrow night." He gave me a hard stare.

I looked at his hand on my shoulder and felt an urge to punch him in his pretty-boy nose but remembered the mission and what was at stake.

"Whatever," I said, brushing his hand off my shoulder.

Navarro smiled, then stepped back and wagged his index finger in the air. "You will win," he said in that same demanding tone he used earlier.

The guy with the topknot started lifting himself from the ground, and when he was in a push-up position, Navarro raised his Italian loafer and stomped the man in the back twice. The already injured man groaned, then dropped flat on the mat.

"I like winners," Navarro said while approaching the bald guy.

The man rested on his knees and elbows and had his head hanging down toward the mat. Navarro exhaled a shout as he kicked the man in his ribcage. The bald guy hollered, then cradled his ribs and fell to his side and coughed while writhing on the mat.

"You're both fired," Navarro said to the men before turning to me. "I really hate losers," he continued.

I folded my arms and opened my mouth. A small yawn came out.

"Am I boring you, Mr. White?"

Kinda, but you're testing my patience more than anything else. "If we're done here, I'd like to get settled in and get some training done," I said.

Navarro smirked. "Sure, this way."

I followed him out of the cage, and Ivan tailed me. We left the gym and walked back into the hall, then toward the main foyer area. As we approached the staircase, I heard a familiar voice call, "Boss."

The group of us looked between the staircase and walking toward us from the front entrance was Snyder with Long following behind him. I kept my eyes on them as they continued across the foyer to us. Snyder glanced at me, then rolled his eyes, but had no surprise reaction to seeing me. *Boss.* It threw me off. The dots weren't connecting. Snyder and Long being there made no sense.

"Yeah, what is it?" Navarro asked Snyder with a hint of irritation in his voice.

"We're all set, but need to talk," Snyder said.

Navarro sighed. "Let's go to my office," he said before turning to Ivan. "Take Mr. White to his room."

Ivan nodded while Navarro, Snyder, and Long walked to the foyer before taking a right and disappearing behind the staircase.

"This way," Ivan said.

I followed him to the opposite side of the house, which was the west wing. We entered a hall similar to the gym's hall. After passing multiple doors on either side, Ivan stopped at a door near the end of the hall on the right.

"This is your room," he said. "Lunch will be in about an

hour. Someone will be by to escort you to the dining room," he concluded before walking away abruptly.

I shrugged, opened the bedroom door, and stepped into an enormous space. A king-sized bed sat centered on the far end wall, and there were two doors on either side behind it. To the left, a sliding balcony door allowed light through. I walked to the door and closed its thick curtain, then walked to the right side of the room and searched the dresser drawers. Inside I found activewear, unopened packs of underwear, sleepwear, jeans, and shirts. It all looked unused. I searched the room for cameras or listening devices but didn't find any. I opened the door on the right side of the bed and discovered a closet and a full bathroom behind the one on the left. Once I was certain there were no surveillance devices in the room, I removed the flip phone and opened it. I located the SMS icon, selected it, and entered the correct password. A message from Deidra displayed. It was good news, but not all good.

CHAPTER
ELEVEN

WE FOUND VARGAS, but he's a bit banged up, the text message said.

I replied with, *Can you talk now?* Twenty seconds later, another message came through, *Yes.* I dialed Deidra's number and waited while the phone rang. After the third ring, she answered.

"Hi Black, how's it going?"

"That all depends."

"What do you mean?"

"How's Vargas?"

"Oh, he's fine. Just a few cuts and bruises. He said Snyder and Long roughed him up a bit, and Ramos took the winnings from your last fight."

"Is that all? He's fortunate."

"Yeah, I'd say he was, cause he mentioned when they arrived at your motel, Ramos told Long to take the car and get rid of him. You can take that to mean what you'd like but sounds like he wanted him dead. Fortunately, Long let Vargas go and we found him five miles west outside of Pleasanton. He also expressed his apologizes for telling them where you were staying. But like I told him, it was good for his cover. Bad guys don't have a sense of loyalty."

Deidra paused. I guess to give me an opportunity to interject, but I said nothing.

"Anyway," she continued. "I'm not putting Vargas back in the field. Can't risk it. So, no more Hector Corrales."

"So, I'm on my own?"

"Yeah, for now, but I'm pulling you out, too."

"I'm good with that."

"It's just too risky. We're still working on locating Ramos' house—any luck finding an address on your side?"

"Hold on," I said as a thought occurred to me. "Yesterday you said you were able to pinpoint Vargas' cell phone. Why can't you do the same with mine?"

"We tried, but it didn't work. Your phone is programmed differently than Vargas'. We should've checked before sending you out with it, but things were moving so fast."

"Well, I guess there's nothing we can do about that now."

"Did you find an address or location for Ramos' place?"

"About that... I'm now with Navarro."

"What? How?"

"I was at Ramos' house training, then he told me to leave with Navarro."

"When? Why—you're at his house?"

"This morning, because he wants me to fight for him, and yes."

"Well, do you know where you are? Did you notice anything unusual about the place?"

"Still in Mexico. It's very large, with maybe fifteen or twenty armed guards."

Deidra sighed into the phone. "Okay, but did you notice any people there? Held against their will?"

"Hostages?"

"Yeah, I guess."

"No, but I've only seen maybe half of this place."

"Alright, just keep an eye out."

"So, what about pulling me out?"

The line went silent. Deidra took in a breath, then slowly exhaled.

"The fight's tomorrow night. Can you stay in just until the fight is over?"

"I'm not sure that's a good idea. I've been trafficked, and who's to say that won't happen again? There may be another fight some scumbag wants me in."

"You'll be fine. We'll find you before then."

"I'm supposed to just take your word for it?"

Deidra scoffed. "What does that mean?"

"This operation is getting messy. I'm getting out the moment I have a chance."

"Don't forget the obstruction charges we have on you, Black."

"I could not care less about those charges, and my patience is about to run out."

"Look here—" Deidra said raising her voice.

"No, you look here," I interrupted. "You're not being straight with me, and I'm tired of being your pawn."

"Black, I just need—"

"You just need to be straight with me," I interrupted again.

She sighed. "I can't tell you everything."

"Well, I'm telling you this, the first opportunity I get, I'm walking away."

"Wait—"

"You'll have to figure another way to find your *question mark*."

"Huh? What do you mean?" Deidra asked.

"The person the DEA is after," I drawled. "The entire reason you had Vargas undercover and sent me in."

"Oh yeah, of course."

The line went silent again. I was thinking. I assumed Deidra was doing the same.

"Okay, Black, I'll level with you," she finally said. "This operation is off the books."

"Figured this much."

"Only myself, Jessica, Vargas, Anson, and you know about it."

"So, there's no backing from the federal government?"

"Not officially."

"And unofficially?"

"We may be riding the coattail of another agency's investigation."

I scoffed a chuckle.

"I have a friend in the FBI we're jointly working with," she continued.

"Unofficially?"

"Yes, but they're backing us."

"Backing you? What exactly are they doing on their end?"

"The FBI has had their investigation open for about six months now. They've even planted an informant inside, according to my friend."

"Do you know who this informant is?"

"I don't know. They wouldn't give me the specifics on that."

"Some friend they are."

"I can understand. The DEA's involvement is unofficial, and they didn't want to jeopardize the safety of their CI, or the investigation."

"I'm sure the FBI knows you sent people in," I said.

"They do."

"Do they know specifics about it?"

"No."

"What are you after?"

Deidra cleared her voice. "What do you mean?"

"I don't understand why this case interests you so much."

Deidra said nothing.

"You're willing to lose your career over an unsanctioned op," I continued. "The question is why."

She remained quiet.

"Who's the FBI investigating specifically?" I asked.

The line went silent for a moment, then Deidra cleared her voice.

"They've been investigating Navarro's criminal activity," she said before exhaling a nervous chuckle.

"There is no *question mark,* is there?" I asked.

She didn't answer.

"I didn't think so," I said. "It makes sense. On the investigative board at your office, you had pictures of Snyder and Long pointing to a question mark as if they worked for the question mark. But I heard Snyder refer to Navarro as boss. That more than likely means both Snyder and Long are working for Navarro. I can understand the FBI and the DEA investigating Navarro for his criminal activities, but what I don't understand is why you'd lie about it. I know your superiors don't know, but does your team know? Does Anson, Jessica, or better yet, Vargas know they're chasing a shadow?"

"Black, it's not like that—"

"Then it's time you start telling me what it's like."

"I didn't know Long and Snyder worked for Navarro."

"Okay, tell me what you do know. Why are you so interested in Navarro?"

Deidra inhaled. "Okay, it's—" she started as three stern knocks hit my room door.

"I have to go," I whispered before ending the call and placing the phone in my pocket.

I walked to the door and when I opened it, Ivan was on the other side with his fist raised, about to knock again.

"What's going on?" I asked him.

"Change of plans," he said while peering over my

shoulder and into the room. "We're having lunch earlier than usual."

I pointed my thumb back at the room. "Okay, let me get—"

"Now."

I shrugged. "Well, let's go then," I said before stepping into the hall and closing the door.

We walked down the hallway, through the foyer area, and into a living room. Standing in the room were Long and Snyder. Next to them stood a guard toting a B&T 9mm submachine gun.

"What's happening here?" I asked, no one in particular.

Snyder just looked at me and squinted while Long lightly hunched his shoulders.

"This way," Ivan said, pointing to a large doorway on the left.

I followed Long and Snyder through it, with Ivan and the guard behind me. On the other side was a spacious dining room with a long-skirted table that sat maybe sixteen. At the head of the table, on the opposite side of the room, Navarro sat with his fingers steepled. I saw the tension in his jaws and around his eyes as he watched us enter the room. Behind him, standing near the corner next to a pair of French glass doors, was another armed guard. The room fell silent, and we all stood like soldiers awaiting our next command.

"Have a seat, gentlemen," Navarro said in a low, direct tone.

I walked to the chair closest to Navarro's left and sat. Ivan sat next to me. Long and Snyder circled the table and sat opposite to me with Snyder closest to Navarro. The guard who followed us in stood at the corner near the doorway.

The table was quiet as Navarro peered at everyone's face. After a few moments, he smiled.

"I figured we should eat early because there's some... business I'd like to discuss," he said.

Snyder's eyebrows crinkled. "What is it, boss?"

Navarro raised his palm as to demand silence. "We'll eat first," he said without looking at Snyder.

Moments later, the maid I saw earlier along with another maid brought us glasses of water with lemon and a plate with chicken quesadillas, salsa, guacamole, and mixed fruit.

"Before I forget," Navarro said to the maid as she was leaving. "Make sure our special guests get a plate."

The maid nodded. "Si, señor."

"Gracias."

We spent the next fifteen minutes eating in silence. I guess no one knew what to say, or what to think, for that matter. When we finished our meals, the maids came back, cleared the dishes, and we sat quietly for a minute while Navarro gazed around the table with a hard stare.

"There's a rat at this table," he said.

Long and Snyder glanced at each other, and both Navarro and Ivan looked at them. In their moment of distraction, I slowly lowered my hand under the table and draped it over my lap and toward my ankle knife holster. I calculated, and the odds didn't look good. Six targets, two at a distance and readily armed, and only four knives. It could be done, but not without making a lot of noise and possibly suffering injuries.

"Does anyone know anything about that?" Navarro continued as he shifted his attention to me.

I shrugged and felt my face muscles create a nonchalant expression while I gently raised my knee and grasped the handle of my knife.

Navarro hunched his shoulders. "So, no one knows anything?" he said before sliding his chair back and standing.

Snyder hunched his own shoulders. "I don't know anything about this, boss," he said while shaking his head.

Navarro nodded. "Interesting. Because I don't know exactly who it is, but a reliable source informed me that I have a rodent in my house, and I believe him."

The table went silent.

"But if I had to guess who it was..." Navarro continued, looking at me.

I kept the nonchalant look on my face while lifting my knife an inch from the holster.

"I'd say it's one of you two," Navarro said as he pointed toward Long and Snyder.

Snyder stood and the two guards approached the table with their guns trained on him.

"I had nothing to do with this," Snyder shouted.

Navarro scoffed. "So, are you saying it's your friend?" he asked while throwing a nod at Long. "I've only known him for a few months, but I've known you for a few years."

Long said nothing, just looked at Navarro and Snyder.

"I'm—I'm not saying it's anyone," Snyder said with his hands raised in a surrender posture. "I just think we all should calm down and not jump to conclusions," he continued before facing me and pointing. "And what about him? You don't know anything about him and you don't suspect him?"

Navarro looked at me. I remained nonchalant, but my knife was out of its holster.

"No," Navarro said, turning back to Snyder. "Like you said, I barely know him. And from the information given to me, this person knew things that only someone who's been around me at least a few times would know."

Snyder eyed Long.

Long hunched his shoulders, "What's going on?" he mouthed.

Snyder turned to Navarro. "I don't know anything about it," he said. "And that's my word."

Navarro stared at him for a moment before turning to the table. "Let's get some fresh air," he said.

I eased my knife back into the holster.

Navarro lifted his hands with his palms facing up.

"Everyone up. Let's go."

The guard closest to the French doors opened them and stepped outside. Everyone at the table stood and followed Navarro through the doors while the other guard followed close behind us. The sunlight warmed my skin, and a breeze hit my face the moment I stepped outside. We stood on a long patio that flowed into a well-manicured backyard, and the yard into an enormous field. Beyond that were mountains as far as the eye could see. Patio furniture sat arranged to our right, with a hot tub and a connecting pool behind it. As we strolled to the opposite end of the patio, I noticed two more guards. One was closer to the house on the left side of the patio, and the other was closer to the backyard to the right of the patio. At the end of the patio, a large rectangular platform with a view of the backyard welcomed us. Navarro stood there, looking toward the mountains while the rest of us huddled in. The two guards who escorted us stepped back and flanked us on either side.

"You know why I like it here so much?" Navarro said. "Not only is it beautiful, but it's quiet, peaceful. No one really bothers me here. Not the local Mexican authorities, at least." He faced the group. "But every now and then, the government goes sticking their nose into business that doesn't concern them. My business." Navarro turned back toward the field and mountains. "Especially, the pesky US government. With all their corruption, you'd think they'd mind their own business." He sighed. "Over there," he said while pointing toward the field.

I followed his finger past the arborvitaes, the perfectly trimmed shrubs, the lush green grass, the beds of flowers, and down an incline to the large dusty, cactus infected field. A helipad and hangar sat near the center. A man opened the hangar doors, and a moment later a cloud of dust rose from the doors and a grinding noise followed by a faint roar struck my ear. The man stepped back as a vehicle rolled from the hangar. It pulled out twenty-five feet from the doors and parked. The dust settled, and I surveyed the piece of machinery. It was an M24 Chaffee. A light-weight tank used during World War II.

Navarro glanced over his shoulder at the tank, then back at us. "She's a beauty, isn't she?" he said, smiling as he did with his dimples pronounced in his cheeks. "Old, but I restored it and made some modifications."

No one replied.

"Perhaps a demonstration," Navarro continued.

I looked at the field and noticed a firing barricade two hundred yards away from the hangar. Figured it'd be the target for his demonstration.

"But we still need a target," Navarro said with his eyes narrowed on Snyder.

Snyder's mouth gaped, and he gently shook his head.

"How many people have you kidnapped, tortured, and killed for me?" Navarro asked him.

"I—I don't know, boss."

"Oh, you don't? Wrong answer," Navarro said before nodding to the armed guard closest to Snyder.

"What?" Snyder hollered.

The guard aimed his gun at Snyder.

"It's not me, boss!"

Navarro shrugged. "That may be true," he said. "But you know the most about me, so you're the biggest risk. Take him to the barricade."

The two guards escorted Snyder through the backyard at gunpoint.

"Boss, please, it's not me!" Snyder pled as they led him toward the field.

Navarro stepped to Long. "You're taking over his responsibilities, got it?"

Long nodded. "Yes, boss," he said, his voice shaky.

"And for future reference, if I ever ask you the question I

just asked him—the answer is always none."

Long nodded again.

"Give me your phone," Navarro said while extending his hand.

Long reached into his pocket and produced a flip phone. Navarro took the phone and scoffed at the sight of it. He then walked to me and extended his hand.

"Phone," he said.

I removed my flip phone and handed it to him.

"These old phones," he said. "I'll get you an upgrade. Now Mr. White, it's about to get very loud and messy out here. In a traumatic way. And since you have to fight for me tomorrow, I don't want you to be around when that happens. I need you focused. So, Ivan will take you back to your room where you'll change, then go to the gym. I'll have a trainer there waiting for you."

I glanced at the field and saw Snyder and the guards approaching the hanger, then saying nothing, I looked Navarro up and down, turned, and walked toward the house. Ivan's footsteps followed behind me.

"Mr. White," Navarro called.

I glanced over my shoulder

"Keep an ear out for the boom," he said, then smirked.

I shrugged. *Not impressed, but you'll be when I get my hands on you*, I thought before cutting my eyes and continuing toward the house with Ivan a few steps behind me.

Ivan and I continued into the house and toward the west wing. As we entered my room's hallway, a door to my left opened and the maid from earlier stepped out with two empty plates in hand. I peeked around her, and a shock tingled up my arms at what I saw. Inside the room was the same tanned, fit lady, and little girl I saw at Ramos' house. I continued walking past without an outward reaction and heard the door shut.

What are they doing here?

CHAPTER
TWELVE

THE QUESTION PUZZLED me until I entered my room. The moment I shut the door in Ivan's face, the answer came to me, and it made me despise Navarro even more. I imagined my hands around his neck, and him begging. When cornered, they always begged or tried to bargain. Navarro looked like a beggar. Figuring my time would be better spent finding a way out and maintaining my cover, I walked to the dresser and removed a pair of sweatpants and a sleeveless workout shirt. As I threw the clothes on the bed, a boom echoed through the room and the house rocked. I shook my head and felt more disdain for Navarro.

I really don't like you, I thought as the image of me choking him came back to mind. Quickly dismissing the thought, I stripped and shrugged into the workout clothes, then exited the room and found Ivan waiting for me at the end of the hall.

He stared at me.

I stopped and stared back.

"The trainer is waiting for you in the gym," he said.

"No kidding," I said.

"Let's go."

"I know where the gym is," I said while walking toward the opposite wing of the house. "I don't need a shadow."

Ivan said nothing, and after a moment I heard his footsteps moving toward the back of the house. Probably going back outside with Navarro and Long. I really didn't care where he was going, only that he wasn't following me. When I made it to the gym, there was only one other person in there other than me. A sturdy man wearing shorts, a Dri-Fit shirt, and a buzz cut, stood at a punching bag throwing jabs. As I approached him, I noticed he had cauliflower ears and a knot on his forehead. He stopped his assault on the bag and turned to face me.

"You must be this Ghost I've been hearing so much about," he said while peeling open his gloves' Velcro straps.

"That's me."

"Alright, I'm your trainer," the man said, placing his gloves together before sticking them under his left armpit and extending his right hand.

We shook.

"Based on what I'm hearing," he started, "we don't have to spend a lot of time on the basics—and we really don't have the time anyway, so I'd like to focus on speed and strength."

"That's the same thing the last trainer said."

"What's that?"

I shrugged. "Nothing."

"Okay, then. Let's start with some stretching."

We spent the next thirty minutes stretching, and an hour and a half after that, punching the bags, tossing the medicine ball, and on the weights. Sprints, stepping drills, and jump rope took up another hour. And with our final hour and a half together, I was in the boxing ring striking the focus pads, then inside the octagon cage grappling.

"You're a natural," the trainer said as we both leaned against the boxing ring, drinking water.

I shrugged.

"You were holding back a lot, but I know this comes easy to you. I was a fighter for a while and have trained many people, but you're the complete package."

"Thanks."

"No really, you should be training me."

I said nothing.

"Tomorrow, after breakfast, I figured we'll do a light training session for two hours and that'll be it. I want you rested for the fight later that evening, alright?"

"Yeah," I said.

"Okay, well I'ma get out of here," the trainer said, hoisting his gym bag's strap over his shoulder. "I'll be back tomorrow."

"You're not staying on the compound?" I asked.

"Nah, man, I stay off site."

I nodded.

"But I'll catch you tomorrow," he said, then walked toward the exit.

I wiped the perspiration from my face, took a sip of my water, then thought for a minute before heading for the exit myself. When I made it halfway to the door, the man with the limp and salt-and-pepper afro entered, rolling a large garbage bin behind him. Large enough for two average-size adults to fit inside. I approached him while he emptied the contents of a trash can near the door into his garbage bin.

"Evening, sir," I said, tossing my plastic bottle into his bin.

He looked at me. "Evening," he said before turning back to his bin.

"If you don't mind me asking, sir, what's your name?"

"I'm the janitor," the man said as he pulled his bin toward the center of the gym.

I followed him. "Even janitors have names."

He stopped near the boxing ring and glanced at me before walking to the ring and picking up some scraps of paper and a couple of empty bottles. He threw them in the garbage bin. "Sam," he said.

"I'm Anthony White."

"Yeah, I heard of you," Sam said as we continued toward the opposite side of the gym. He stopped near the punching bags and looked at me. "That's not your real name, is it?"

"I beg your pardon?"

Sam smiled. "They don't call you Anthony White in the ring, do they? I heard you move like a ghost."

I smiled back. "Yeah, in the ring they call me Ghost."

Maintaining his smile, Sam nodded, then picked up a small garbage can and tipped it into his bin.

"How long have you worked here?" I asked.

He looked up and squinted. "About four years," he answered before wheeling his squeaky garbage bin along.

"Do you like it here?"

"I guess there're worse places."

"Maybe. How did you end up working here?"

Sam stopped wheeling the bin and turned to me. "That's a long story."

I said nothing.

"You have a lot of questions, Mr. White. Do you mind me asking you one?" he said as his eyes moved from my face to the top of my head.

I shrugged.

"Where do you get your haircut?"

"That's an interesting question."

"It's an interesting haircut."

"What, you looking for a barber?"

"Maybe. I sure do need one," Sam said as he patted his fro and pulled the garbage bin behind himself.

I stood and watched, connecting the dots in my head while he made his way toward the octagon cage. After a few seconds, I grinned, then turned and exited the gym. I made it to the end of the hall before hearing heavy, rapid footsteps approach me from around the corner. To avoid a collision, I stopped, and a second later, an armed guard faced me.

"The boss needs to see you," he said.

"Okay. Let me shower and I'll be right there," I said.

"Now. You can clean up after."

I was really getting tired of being told what to do. It felt like I was back in the military, and I didn't like it. My patience was wearing thin, and I needed to take action before it cost me, and Navarro too, for that matter. But since I preferred the scenario where it only cost Navarro, I maintained my cool and played along.

"Alright," I said with a shrug.

"This way," the guard said while pointing to his left.

We walked back toward the west wing, passed between the staircase, made a right in the foyer, and landed in a short hall. At the end of the hallway waited large, wooden double doors. The guard opened one side of the door and waved me through. I walked inside and a potpourri scent hit my face. Navarro sat in a leather, executive office chair behind a hearty desk made of maple wood. He was on the phone but waved the guard away and gestured for me to take a seat in one of the two chairs facing his desk. The guard stepped out of the room and closed the door while I walked across the hard-wood floor and took a seat in the chair to Navarro's left. While Navarro listened into the phone, I continued to scan the room. Behind him was a large bookshelf and on either side of it were windows framing the last glimmer of daylight as dusk set in. To my far right was a gun shelf made of the same maple as Navarro's desk. It was closed, and I assumed locked, but through the glass I saw a few rifles and handguns.

"Yes, I understand—" Navarro said into the phone.

I continued to scan the top of his desk and saw something I'd seen before. My phone, and next to it, rested Long's phone.

"I promise," Navarro said to the person on the other side

of the line. "This will be one of the most amazing, if not the most amazing, displays of talent you've ever seen in a fight. It'll be well worth your money."

I reclined in the chair. Navarro glanced at me, then listened some more.

"Absolutely. I'll see you tomorrow night," he said before pressing at his phone's screen and placing it face down on his desk. "Sorry for the wait, Mr. White. That was a… customer service call."

I said nothing.

"So, how was your training session?" he asked while placing mine and Long's phone into a desk drawer and locking it with a small key.

"Productive. I enjoyed it."

"Good. You feel you'll be ready for tomorrow? That you'll win?"

"I think so."

Navarro stared at me before leaning back in his chair. "I need you to know, Mr. White. There's a lot of money on the table for me, and I'd hate to waste some of it on more ammunition for my tank."

For a moment, I entertained the thought of jumping over the desk and wringing Navarro's neck. I could be gone by the time anyone noticed, but then again, I'm sure Navarro ordered the guards to keep me on the compound, so I wouldn't be able to leave quietly.

"I'll win. Just have my money," I said.

"You better."

"Are we done here? I have a big day tomorrow, and I'd like to get some rest."

Navarro pointed at the door. "I'll have the maid bring you your dinner."

I stood and walked toward the door but turned when I made it halfway. "That woman and child down the hall from me—"

"Yes. It's Ramos' wife and daughter," Navarro said as he also stood. "How else would I've convinced him to let you fight for me?"

I shrugged. "I don't know. Maybe money."

Navarro crinkled his nose and shook his head. "Nah. This way's much cheaper."

"Why keep them? I'm going to fight for you."

"Insurance. I wouldn't want Ramos thinking he could storm my compound before the fight without there being some serious repercussions."

"What's to stop him from storming it once he gets his family back?"

Navarro walked from around the desk and stood where I sat minutes before. "If he gets his family back," he said, before pausing and staring at me. "After the connections and money I make from this fight tomorrow, Ramos would be insane to show up at my doorstep."

I nodded.

Navarro shifted his weight between his legs, folded his arms, then squinted. "Why do you ask?" he said. "You have a problem with the way I do business?"

Of course I do, you piece of crap. Any real man would.

I shook my head. "No. It's just I don't usually involve women and children in my business," I said before smiling, and pointing my index finger at him as if I was pressing an invisible button in the air. "But you have an interesting way of handling business. And as long as I get paid, I don't care."

I noticed a grin cross Navarro's face as I turned and walked to the door, and when I opened it a slit, I heard him say, "I'll get what's coming to me, and you'll be a wealthy man, Mr. White."

You're definitely going to get what's coming to you, I thought as I exited the office without looking back.

The guard stood just outside the room. I brushed past him on my way out of the hall before cutting through the foyer, then to the west wing, and finally to my room. Once inside, I removed a change of clothes from the drawer and took a shower. After drying off and slipping into my clean clothes, I sat on the bed with my thoughts.

Yep, definitely another fine mess.

Four brisk knocks came from my door. I figured it was the maid with my dinner, but when I opened the door, I discovered I was only half right. Sam stood at the door with a covered dish in hand.

"Your dinner," he said.

I looked at him.

"I told the maid that I'd bring it to you," he said.

I shrugged and took the covered dish from him. "Thanks," I said.

"Can I have a word with you?"

"Sure," I answered while walking to the bed and placing the dish on top of it.

Sam stepped in and closed the door behind himself.

"So, what do you want to talk about?" I asked.

He limped toward me and stopped an arm's reach away. "I know you're working for the DEA," he said.

CHAPTER
THIRTEEN

THE ROOM WENT silent, and after a few seconds, I chuckled.

"And how would you know that?" I asked.

"Let's just call it a hunch," Sam said.

I raised my eyebrows, because I had a *hunch* of my own.

"Let's say I am. Why are you interested?" I asked.

"I'd like to help you."

"Why?"

"Let's just say… I don't like Navarro."

"Okay. Can you get me into his office?"

Sam winced. "Wait. Just like that, you trust me?" he asked.

"Yeah, I'm pretty sure I can trust you. Is there a reason I shouldn't?"

"No. Just thought it'd be harder to convince you."

I poked my lips and shook my head. "Nope. So, can you get me in?"

"I don't have a key, but there's not much security on this wing late at night and he may leave his office door unlocked."

"I should be able to pick the lock either way," I said.

Sam shrugged. "Okay."

"I didn't notice an alarm system in the foyer or in the office, but are there any I should be concerned about?"

Sam shook his head.

"Good, should be easy then." I thought for a second. "Down this hall," I said. "There's a woman and a little girl—"

"Yeah, I know. That scumbag is using them as hostages."

"Are there any others like them?"

"What do you mean, like them?"

"Hostages."

"No, not that I know of."

I nodded.

"What are you thinking?" Sam asked.

"I'm thinking I don't enjoy seeing innocent people get hurt, and I want to help them escape."

"Taking down Navarro will help with that."

"Does Navarro look like the type who'll go down quietly?"

Sam shrugged his eyebrows and shook his head. "No. He's a coward, so he'll take whoever he can down with him."

"Exactly. What do you know about the trainer I was working with earlier?"

"Seems like a nice man. Has a family. Why?"

"What does he drive?"

"A gray BMW SUV, tinted windows, sporty rims. He takes good care of it, and it's an easy car to recognize. When the guards see him coming, they usually just wave him through."

"Where does he normally park?"

"Near the east wing, close by the gym. Why—what's up?"

"Do you normally wheel that large garbage bin inside the main house?"

Sam shrugged. "Yeah," he said with his eyes squinted.

"The hostage, the woman, are you two on talking terms?"

"Yeah, the few times I took them food or linen or clothes, she'd talk to me. I hate seeing women and children suffer, so I tried to be especially kind to them."

"What time's breakfast tomorrow?"

"Nine. What's with all the questions?"

"I have a plan, but I'm gonna need your help."

I spent the next ten minutes explaining my plan to Sam. He seemed to understand it and had no protest, so I felt it was solid.

"Simple enough," Sam replied with a nod.

"I'm thinking with your leg you should probably go with them," I said. "When Navarro learns what happened, things may get... pretty loud around here."

"No, I'm staying. I want to see that scumbag get nailed."

"You sure?"

"Positive."

"It's your choice, but I'll say at least have a place to hide in case things get heated."

"Hide?"

I shrugged.

Sam grunted. "Whatever," he said. "I better get out of here before someone suspects something."

He walked to the door, and I followed.

"Oh, before I forget," I said, "what's the address here?"

Sam gave me the address before leaving the room. I walked to my bed, removed the cover from my dish, inspected my food, and ate. After, I searched the room for something I could use as a lock pick. I hoped to find something lying around in the main area, or the bathroom, or the closet, but there was nothing. I stood thinking for a moment before removing one of the dresser's drawers and placing it on the floor. Reaching my arm into the space, I felt a tiny, thin metal strip running horizontally across the back of the dresser. A smile crossed my face as I bent the strip until it was weak enough for me to snap a piece off. I bent that piece into two, then shaped them the best I could. Once done, I replaced the dresser drawer, set my mental alarm clock, and took a nap.

When I woke two hours later, I put on my shoes and strapped my knife holsters around my ankle before grabbing the two strips of metal and heading toward the door. I opened it an inch and peeked into the hall. It was quiet, so I stuck my head out and looked both ways. It was clear. While exiting my room, I gently closed the door behind me, then crept down the dark hallway. Once I reached the end of the hall, I pressed my back against the wall and glanced around the corner. No one was in sight. I darted around the corner and hustled into the foyer area as quickly and quietly as I could, listening for any noise out of the ordinary. Silence. I continued between the staircase and into the main foyer. As I made my way toward Navarro's office hallway, I heard voices on the other side of the front door.

It sounded like idle chitchat coming from some guards, but I figured I came too far to stop, so I continued into the hall and to Navarro's office, where I found the door locked. Kneeling, I inserted the metal pieces from inside my dresser into the door's keyhole. After a couple of minutes of fiddling with the mechanism, the lock clicked, and I opened the door. At that same moment, the door at the front of the house opened and laughter flowed from the foyer. I zipped into the office and closed the door just enough so I could peek through. The silhouette of a soldier stepped into the foyer. He exchanged words with someone outside the door before shutting it and walking toward the staircase. As the guard disappeared from my sight, I closed the door completely and locked it before circling Navarro's desk and kneeling at the drawer.

I pulled the handle, and to my surprise, the drawer slid open. Inside, my phone sat on top of a notepad next to Long's phone. I removed my phone, flipped it opened, then checked for messages, but found none. After clicking the SMS icon and entering my password, I immediately typed, *Navarro took*

my phone. I snuck into his office to use it, so don't have much time.
I sent it, then typed, *Snyder is dead. Navarro killed him. He thought he was an informant.* As I was typing, a message came through.

Okay. Not good then. He's on high alert.

I typed the address Sam had given me. *This is the address.*

Great! Now you need to get out.

I'm working on it, I typed, then paused and thought. *But Navarro has 2 hostages,* I sent and waited for Deidra's reply.

Whip, came through immediately.

I quietly chuckled.

Who? she corrected.

Ramos' wife and daughter.

That bastard used them as leverage.

Exactly.

You need to get out.

With that last text message, I heard footsteps in the hall approaching the office. I gently closed the desk drawer and sat with my back against it as the office doorknob rattled. Seconds later, the door opened and someone entered the room. Three steps knocked against the hardwood floor, then stopped near the desk. Judging by the strut, I knew it was a guard, and could feel them only feet away. I slowly extended my hand toward my knife holster. A moment later, the man walked back to the door and left the office. I peeped over the desk as the door shut behind him.

Have to go, I texted Deidra.

Be careful.

Got it. Signing off, I sent before deleting our conversation and placing the phone back into the drawer and sliding it closed.

I nudged the office door open and peeked out. Seeing the hallway was clear, I exited the room and softly closed the door. I gave the knob a twist just to make sure it locked, and while crouched, I hurried down the hall. I continued through the foyer, between the staircase, through my hall, and into my room. After searching the room and finding nothing out of the ordinary, I hid the metal pieces I used as a lock pick inside the dresser behind the drawer, then kicked off my shoes, unstrapped my knife holsters, and went to bed.

The next morning, I woke to birds chirping outside my room. I eased from the bed and walked toward the balcony door. Pulling back the curtain, light entered the room, and the birds stopped chirping. The room clock showed 7:09 a.m. It was later than I normally woke, but then again, I was always in different times zones and the past few days had been anything but normal. I yawned and stretched on my way to the bathroom, where I washed my face and brushed my teeth. Returning to the main bedroom area, I walked to the dresser, removed some workout clothes, and shrugged into them before making my bed and leaving the room. I figured I'd head to the gym in hope of running into Sam, but there was no sign of him on my way there. When I entered the gym, I saw the trainer fiddling with something inside his duffle bag. The sound of keys jingling hit my ear as he shook the bag and zipped it up.

He turned and faced me as I approached him. "Good morning," he said. "I was just on my way to get you."

"Good morning," I said. "Well, now you don't have to."

The trainer rested his hands on his hips and nodded. "How are you feeling?"

"Hopeful."

The trainer chuckled. "Well, that's a good thing. Whattaya say we stretch and warm-up before breakfast?"

"Let's do it."

We spent the next hour stretching and performing push-ups and sit-ups. As we ended our session with some shadow boxing drills, Ivan entered the gym.

"Breakfast is almost ready," he said before immediately turning and leaving.

The trainer shrugged. "Well, I guess we better get ready for breakfast. Dry off and grab some water. I gotta use the head," he said before exiting the gym with his water bottle in hand.

I grabbed a towel and wiped my face, then took a swig of water. While glancing over my shoulder, I walked to the trainer's duffle bag. I unzipped it and stuck my hand inside. After a few seconds of feeling around, I removed a set of keys. Noticing one key had the BMW symbol engraved on it, I zipped the duffle bag and placed the keys in my pocket before exiting the gym. I made it to the end of the hall when I heard a door in the hallway open. The trainer exited, looked toward the gym, then in the opposite direction at me. I nodded. He nodded back. Then the two of us walked to the same dining room where I ate lunch the day before. Ivan and Long sat at the table across from one another, eating. The seats next to them were empty, and covered dishes rested in front of them. I chose a seat on the same side as Long, while the trainer sat next to Ivan.

"Where's the boss?" the trainer asked.

"He's taking care of some business," Ivan said between chews. "He'll be here shortly."

I removed the cover from my dish and caught a whiff of eggs, sausage, tortillas, salsa, and mixed fruit. Ten minutes into the meal, Ivan finished and left the table. Three minutes after that, Long did the same, leaving me and the trainer alone at the table. And at the fifteen-minute mark, I finished my meal, but Navarro entered the dining room.

"How are we looking?" he said, while clapping his palms and rubbing his hands together.

I said nothing, just sipped my water.

The trainer smiled. "He's quite the fighter," he said to Navarro, before glancing at me. "I believe he's more than experienced enough for Ken."

"Good," Navarro said. "Because there's a lot riding on this fight."

"Understood. After we finish breakfast, we'll review some videos."

"Okay. Have to run—lots to do for tonight," Navarro said, before sharing his gaze between the trainer and me, and walking out of the dining room.

"Ken?" I said to the trainer.

"Yeah. We'll review some of his footage," he said before taking a bite of his food.

"Okay," I said, while standing from the table. "I'll be in the gym."

The trainer nodded with a mouth full of food, and I left the dining room. When I arrived in the gym's hallway, Sam stood at the corner with his large garbage bin next to him.

With my head on a swivel, I walked to him.

"Here," I whispered, handing him the keys I took from the trainer's bag. "Remember to tell her to call the number I gave you."

Sam placed the keys in his pocket. "Got it. I explained the plan to her when I took them breakfast this morning."

"Good. She's aware."

"Yeah, but it's still a little risky. We're trusting the trainer will—"

"He will," I said. "He's a family man. Besides, I've already given the DEA the address for here. With what's coming, it's more of a risk for them to stay here."

"You may be right."

"I'm guessing he'll be leaving within the next few hours. Try to get it done and the keys back in my hand or his gym bag by then."

"Copy that," Sam said as he walked toward the main living area, wheeling the garbage bin behind himself.

"Be careful," I said.

He stopped, peered over his shoulder at me, then nodded

before turning back and continuing to walk. I went to the gym, and fifteen seconds after I entered, the trainer walked in with a circular disk in hand. I figured it was a DVD.

"Follow me," he said on his way toward the back of the gym.

We walked to where the octagon cage was. In the east corner, a forty-inch flat screen TV and a thin DVD player hung flush on the wall. The trainer walked to the screen, pressed a button on the side, sparking light on the display and turning the screen blue. He then pressed a button on the DVD player. The player buzzed open. He inserted the disk, then the player buzzed closed and hummed as the word play displayed on the flat screen. The trainer crouched under the screen and picked up a remote before stepping backward and fixing his attention on the screen.

A few seconds later, a man attacking a punching bag displayed on the TV. The man had dark-brown hair in a crew cut. His frame was muscular but lean, and his face was smooth, with an unassuming look.

"My opponent?" I said. "His strikes are fast and accurate."

"Yeah. Ken the K.O. King."

I shook my head.

"What, you don't like it?"

"No, and for many reasons."

The video faded into a different scene, showing Ken squaring off against a large man with a bodybuilder's physique. The bulky man swung twice at Ken. A wild right, followed by an even wilder left. As the big man cocked back for a third punch, Ken delivered two rapid kicks to the side of the man's kneecap. The big guy dropped to his other knee and Ken hit him with a haymaker. Spit gushed from the man's mouth as Ken jumped and finished him with a knee to the face. The big man descended backward, then smacked into the mat.

The trainer scoffed. "He's good," he said while nodding.

The video switched to another scene, and Ken was performing the same jumping knee attack he used in the previous fight on a bald, muscular guy.

The trainer paused the video. "But every fighter has a weakness," he said before pointing the remote back at the TV and pressing play.

The screen displayed Ken ending a sequence of fights with the same jumping knee attack he executed in the previous fight.

"He likes that move," I said.

"Yeah. It's one of his weaknesses."

We watched the film for ten more minutes, exploring Ken's techniques, habits, and potential weaknesses. Once we were done, the trainer turned off the TV, and we went to the center of the gym and performed a series of drills and exercises. An hour later, sour scented and salty tasting beads of sweat covered my face. We took a break and, as I wiped my face with my towel, the trainer reached into his duffle bag and stirred his arm around. His eyebrows furrowed, and he cocked his head to the side while looking at me.

"Where is it?" he asked.

CHAPTER
FOURTEEN

MY HEART SKIPPED a beat, but I kept a straight face.

"Where's what?" I asked with a shrug.

The trainer scanned around the area near his duffle bag. "My water bottle," he said.

I squinted, then thought for a second before raising my eyebrows. "Check the bathroom."

The trainer closed his eyes and tilted his head back. "Oh yeah. I forgot I left it there," he said. "I'll be back." He jogged to the door and exited the gym.

I exhaled, then went to the door myself and peeked into the hall. I hoped to see Sam, but he wasn't there. *Just stick to the plan,* I thought, while ducking back inside the gym. I walked to a punching bag and threw six jabs. On my seventh jab, the trainer entered the gym with his water bottle in hand. I glanced at him, then continued assaulting the bag as he walked over. We then spent forty-five minutes running through a few more drills before concluding for the day.

"That's it," the trainer said while wiping his face with his towel. "I want you to rest until the fight tonight."

"Will you be there?" I asked.

The trainer shook his head. "No. I just train."

The gym door opened and Sam entered, wheeling the large garbage bin behind him.

About time.

He walked to a garbage receptacle near the front and looked inside it.

The trainer slapped me on my shoulder. "Well, I'm heading out," he said while walking toward his duffle bag.

Gotta' stall him.

I followed behind the trainer. Sam paused and looked at us, and just when I opened my mouth, the trainer stopped and turned.

"I forgot the DVD," he said with his index finger pointed toward the ceiling.

He brushed past me and made his way toward the opposite end of the gym. I beckoned Sam over with a small wave of my hand. The older gentleman hustled toward me while I glanced over my shoulder to make sure the trainer still had his back to us. Sam handed me the keys and made his way back toward his garbage bin. He was quiet and fast. I almost forgot he had a limp. Keeping an eye on the trainer's back, I stepped to his duffle and eased the keys inside near the bottom of the bag. Sam nodded at me, and I nodded back. The old man then moved his bin toward another garbage container in the gym. The trainer was at the DVD player. He glanced at me, and I just stood and watched him. A few minutes later, he made his way back over to me, grabbed his duffle bag, and we exited the gym together. When we made it to the end of the hall, the trainer used his left thumb to point to the left.

"I'm this way," he said before moving his duffle bag from his right hand to his left and extending me his right hand.

I shook it.

"Good luck," he said.

"Thanks."

"Any time," he said before walking away and disappearing around a corner.

I walked back inside the gym. Sam was making his way toward the door with the garbage bin rumbling behind him.

"We're good?" I asked him.

Sam exhaled as if he was holding a breath he didn't know he had. "Yeah, we're good."

"You should've gone with them."

"I said I'm staying. Now watch out. I want to make sure he makes it through the gate with no problem."

"I'll go with you."

"They'll know something's up if you're shadowing me."

"I was planning on keeping my distance. You just signal to me when they've made it out."

Sam cocked his head to the side and hunched his shoulders before wheeling the garbage bin out of the gym and into the hall. I waited ten seconds, then followed. As I stepped into the hall, I caught a glimpse of the garbage bin as Sam turned the corner. I walked down the hall, made a left, and continued behind Sam toward the west wing. When we were halfway to the foyer area, Sam stopped at a window near the front of the house. I knelt and pretended to tie my shoe while he looked out the window. After a few seconds, he glanced at me and nodded. I returned the gesture, then stood and walked past him and toward the foyer. While passing through the foyer, I saw Ivan standing behind the staircase, near the hall where my room was located. He stared at me with cold eyes and folded arms.

I stopped in front of him. "Can I help you?" I said. "You're kinda in my way."

He said nothing, just looked at me. I looked at him. We stayed that way for a good five seconds before he finally opened his mouth.

"Come with me," he said, brushing past on his way toward the front door. "We're going for a ride."

I pivoted in his direction. "Don't have time for a ride. I have a fight tonight."

"I wasn't asking," Ivan said while opening the front door.

Two armed guards entered and crowded on either side of him. Both stared at me with their submachine guns in hand.

I felt tension around my neck and in my jaw. "What's this?" I said.

"No questions. Let's go," Ivan said.

"No."

Ivan glared at me.

"Does the boss know about this ride?" I asked.

Ivan glanced at the floor before moving his eyes back to me.

I'll take that as a no.

"Let's go," he said again.

I thought for a second and figured although it was risky, it could be my way out. It couldn't be any riskier than having a stare-off with three men, two armed with machine guns.

"Just have me back in time to get some rest before the fight," I said, walking across the foyer toward the men.

I looked to my left and saw Sam peeking at the group of us while fiddling with his garbage bin. His wide eyes seemly asking me the question, is everything all right?

I answered yes with a wink while passing Ivan and the two armed guards on my way outside. An SUV was waiting out front. I stopped at the vehicle until I heard Ivan's voice from behind me.

"In the back."

I entered the back passenger side. Ivan sat in the front passenger seat, and one guard sat behind the wheel while the other sat in the back opposite me. From a tactical perspective, I was happy with the seating arrangement. If they were to make a move, the guard in the back was within reaching distance. I'd just have to keep a close eye on his hands. The driver would be mostly occupied with driving, and if Ivan wanted to get in on the action, he'd have to turn around in his seat. The guard pulled the gearshift into drive, and I had already played twelve potential scenarios in my head on how I would escape if they tried something. All ended with me unharmed and them seriously hurt or dead. Except three. In the first of those three, we were all dead. The second, I was badly hurt. And in the third, I was dead. Nine out of twelve unscathed, I was good with those odds.

The SUV hummed down the driveway and when we reached the security hut, the man at the wheel waved to the guard standing near the shack, and a moment later the wrought iron gate clanked, then slid open.

We drove for fifteen minutes, and I paid close attention to the passing landmarks and turns we made. I also paid close attention to the three men in the car with me. After another half a mile of driving, the SUV veered off the main road and onto a dirt road. The vehicle bumped along the inclined, dust-filled road for two more minutes before circling and parking in the direction we came. As the dust cleared from around the SUV, I looked out the driver's side window and saw the edge of a cliff.

Ivan adjusted in his seat and I felt the pressure from his movement. "Out," he said, peering over his left shoulder.

I opened the door and stepped out, and as everyone else opened their doors, I removed one of my knives from its holster and tucked it into the back of my pants before covering it with the hem of my shirt.

Ivan stepped out of the car and nodded toward the cliff's edge. "That way," he said.

A small whirlwind of sand swirled at my feet when I circled the back of the vehicle and walked toward the edge. Ivan followed behind me, and the two guards stood at the SUV with their machine guns draped over their shoulders. I stopped ten feet from the edge and turned, putting Ivan and me face-to-face, three feet apart.

"Some information has been brought to my attention." he said.

"Congratulations," I replied.

He smirked. "I've learned something interesting about your friend Hector Corrales."

"Let me stop you there. I have no friends. Especially someone I've only met a few days ago."

Ivan scoffed. "Whatever he is to you, you're associated."

"He was a means for me to get paid. Just like Ramos, and now, just like your boss."

"Either way, I've learned he's working with the DEA."

Great, I thought before shrugging. "Okay. What does that have to do with me?"

Ivan smirked again. "If he's with the DEA, why should I believe you're not?"

"I don't care what you believe."

Ivan inhaled, then released a long exhale.

"I just want to make money, and you're getting in the way of that."

"So, it's just about money for you?"

"Yeah. Just like it is for your boss. And since he doesn't even know I'm here, you're playing with his money, too."

"My job is to protect Mr. Navarro. Even if it means losing some money."

"You think you're protecting him by trying to intimidate me out here in the middle of nowhere?"

"Do you work for the DEA?"

"The only person I work for is myself," I answered before walking past him and toward the SUV. "I have a fight tonight. I'd like to get back and get some rest," I said with my back to him.

"Hold it," he said.

I stopped and one of the guards approached me with his palm out and his other hand holding his submachine gun. Ivan's footsteps tapped behind me. I turned and faced him.

"We go when I say we go," he said.

"I don't work for you."

"Let's get one thing straight—"

"Unlike your nose," I said.

Ivan growled and reached for me. As he did, I grabbed his hand, twisted, then lifted his wrist. The big man hunched his shoulders and sighed a grunt of pain. The guard closest to us stepped forward, fumbling to bring his machine gun to bear. Maintaining my hold on Ivan's wrist, I pushed the burly man into the guard. The guard clipped Ivan's shoulder and spun toward me while Ivan stumbled to the ground. I grabbed the spinning guard from behind, removed his sidearm, and pointed the pistol at his head. Clenching his submachine gun, I aimed it toward Ivan and the other guard who had only just then trained his gun on me. It all happened too fast for him to respond quickly enough.

"Don't move," I told the guard in my grips.

Ivan was on one knee, his pant leg covered in reddish orange dirt.

"Drop the guns," the guard said to me.

"No. You drop yours, or I'll shoot him," I said while tapping the muzzle of the pistol against the temple of the guard I held. I flicked the submachine gun at Ivan. "And him, too," I continued.

The guard pursed his lips and kept his gun on me, but after a moment, he lowered it.

"Good," I said. "Now toss it over the cliff."

He walked to the edge of the cliff and tossed the gun over.

"And your sidearm," I said.

The guard sighed before hesitantly throwing his pistol over. I swung the submachine to my side, then pushed the guard I held toward Ivan. With both guns aimed at the group of men, I eased to the SUV. The front driver's side door hung open an inch, and the keys were still in the ignition. The three men watched me as I opened the door, tossed the submachine gun in the front passenger seat and started the car with the pistol trained on them. When the engine turned over, I slid in behind the wheel.

Ivan's nostrils flared, and his eyebrows arched downward. "You've made a big mistake," he said.

"You started it," I said before giving him a hard stare. "And if you point or order a gun to be pointed at me again— you'll be the one going over the ledge," I said before shutting the door, peeling off, and watching the group of men disappear behind a wall of dust from my rearview mirror.

I drove the same route back to the house, but first stopped outside a small town and parked off the road to think. I thought about making my way to the border and back to Texas. But then I remembered I didn't have my passport with me and thought about how I ever entered Mexico without one. With no documents and Navarro being so connected, I concluded my best option was to go back to the house and maintain my cover. When I arrived at the house, the guard at the security hut motioned for me to roll down the window. I did as instructed. He squinted while craning toward the window and scanning the front and back seats.

"Where are the others?" he asked me.

"They're on their way," I said.

The man stepped back from the vehicle and stared at me. He walked back to the hut, and the gate opened. As I drove past, I saw the guard talking into his walkie talkie. He probably figured it was better to let me through, regardless if something was wrong or not. That way, I was confined to the compound. I continued down the driveway and parked the SUV in the same spot it sat prior to my ride with Ivan and the gang. I exited the vehicle with the engine turned off and the keys still in the ignition, then hiked up the steps and entered the house. As the door shut behind me, the barrel of a B&T 9mm submachine gun rose to my face.

CHAPTER
FIFTEEN

A SECURITY GUARD stood with his gun trained on me. Navarro, standing a few feet behind him, squinted, then widened his eyes.

"It's White, the fighter," he said to the security guard.

The guard lowered his gun while looking me up and down and releasing a sigh.

Navarro brushed past the guard and stepped to me. "Where have you been?" he asked.

"Went for a drive with Ivan," I said.

Navarro hunched his shoulders. "Okay. Is he with you?" he said while gently shaking his head and opening the door.

I glanced back and saw Navarro looking outside the door and scanning the front of the house. A moment later, the door slapped closed and Navarro walked to me.

"Where's Ivan?" he asked, hunching his shoulders again.

I shrugged. "He decided to... take in the sights," I answered. "Said he'll be here a little later."

Navarro fixed on me for a moment. I could see the wheels turning in his head. Should he believe me? If I had motivations outside of making money, why would I come back? His face painted several questions. Where was Ivan really? After a good ten seconds, he pivoted to the guard.

"Call Ivan—see where he is—and ask him why I don't have security guards out front."

"Sí, Señor," the guard said before walking away and disappearing behind the staircase.

"So, Mr. White," Navarro said. "Where did Ivan take you on this drive?"

I winced. "Oh, he didn't tell you? I thought for sure he would've told you."

Navarro rolled his eyes to the right and sighed.

"But anyhow," I continued. "He drove me up this cliff. At the top was a magnificent view." I stopped and waited to see Navarro's response.

He jerked his head forward, widened his eyes, and opened his hands. "Okay, then what? He didn't drive you there for you two to have a picnic—what happened?"

"We parked, got out of the car, then talked," I said, before stopping again on purpose.

"Talked about what?" Navarro said in an impatience tone.

"He mentioned something about the DEA. I wasn't paying too much attention."

"DEA?" Navarro uttered while looking at the ceiling.

"What? He didn't tell you?"

Navarro looked at me but said nothing.

I shrugged. "Well, he tried to tie me to whatever crap he was spewing from his mouth about the DEA. I didn't appreciate it."

"And then?"

"We had an exchange of words—things got heated—and now he'll need an Uber to get back home."

Navarro cuffed his chin. "So, you got the upper hand on Ivan and decided to come back here. Why?" he said.

"What do you mean, why? I'm looking at a big payday," I said before narrowing my sights on Navarro and cocking my head to the side. "Or did you have other plans, like not paying me?" I wagged my index finger in the air. "That wouldn't be wise, because I wouldn't go quietly," I said, laying it on thick.

Navarro stared at the floor for a moment and chuckled before looking at me with a smile on his face. "Mr. White, there are no other plans. Our deal is our deal. I'm just trying to locate my general and understand how you, a mere fighter, got the best of him. Maybe you should be my general."

I hunched my shoulders, raised my eyebrows, and pursed my lips as if I was considering his offer. "Let's see how our first deal goes, then we'll cross that bridge," I said.

"Fair enough," Navarro said in a dry tone.

The security guard entered the foyer and walked to Navarro.

"Ivan says he has Cortez and Gara with him, and that he'll be back soon," the guard said.

Navarro nodded.

"I'll cover the front until they return, señor," the guard concluded.

"So, it was you, Ivan, and two other members of my security staff at that cliff?" Navarro said to me.

I shrugged. "Yeah, there were two other guys there."

"Interesting. Mr. White, you have a big fight tonight. You should get some rest. I'll have the maid bring you lunch."

I turned and walked toward the staircase. On my way, I heard Navarro whispering to the guard, and as I turned toward my hall, I saw Navarro saying something in the man's ear.

This is going to be an interesting night.

I went to my room and lay in my bed with my thoughts for twenty minutes before five knocks struck my door. On the other side stood Sam with a covered dish. I let him in before peeking into the hall to make sure he was alone. I shut the door and locked it while Sam placed the covered dish on the bed.

"I told the cook I was heading this way, so I'd drop your plate off," he said.

"How nice of you. I think you should seriously reconsider staying here."

Wrinkles crossed Sam's forehead.

"Ivan knows the DEA is investigating Navarro," I said. "And that's an agent only one degree separated from him."

"That's not good."

"No, it's not. And he's extremely ticked at me."

"Why?"

"I held him along with a couple of guards at gunpoint, then left them stranded."

"How? Why would you do that?"

"I took their guns. They started it."

Sam sighed. "Things are heating up, but I'm still staying," he said.

"That's not a good idea."

"I think you should worry more about yourself. After your fight tonight, you'll either be imprisoned as their cash cow or killed."

"Yeah, I figured this much, but there's a third option," I said while walking past Sam and to the bed. "Any suspicion about the girls?"

Sam shook his head. "No one appears more the wiser."

"Good. My contact back at the DEA has the address here, and I'm sure they'll have a team put together to raid this place tonight. So, I want you to look for a way out—"

"I told you I'm not leaving. I'm not going anywhere until I see this bastard get what he deserves."

"Even at the cost of your life?"

Sam stared at me but said nothing.

"I'm sure you have someone that cares about you. At least one, right?"

Sam continued to stare and remained silent.

"Trust me," I said. "When the bullets start flying, you don't want to be around with your leg in the condition it is."

"I'm staying," Sam said. "That's final."

I shook my head, then shrugged. "Okay, but find a place to hide just in case," I said before removing the cover from the dish and inhaling the steamy fumes of rice, beans, salsa, and mixed fruit.

"Done," Sam said before pivoting and walking toward the door. When he reached the door, he turned in my direction. "What's the third option?"

I knew what he was asking but didn't answer.

"I mentioned they'll imprison or kill you. You said there was a third option—what is it?"

I fixed on Sam's face. "I burn this place down along with Navarro's entire operation."

Sam's eyes widened, but he said nothing. He knew I was serious. He knew I was the type of man who meant what I said. Without another word, he nodded and exited the room. I turned to my food, ate, placed the covered dish on the floor, then stretched out on the bed and closed my eyes.

An hour later, I woke to the sound of footsteps rapidly stomping in the hall. My doorknob rattled as I sprang from the bed. The door swung open and Ivan rushed inside. His eyes bulged, and he gritted his teeth while glaring at me. I scoffed and shrugged as the big guy hurled himself in my direction with his palms opened and aimed at my neck. I always liked waiting until my opponents were close before making a move. As a fast and accurate fighter, that's always the best play, because the opponent thinks they have you, so there's a moment of hesitation while their mind slips into performing their next move before fully executing the previous move. I thrive in that moment. When the burly man's hands were inches from my neck, I side-stepped to my right, snaked my left hand between his arms to cuff the back of his neck, then clenched his right arm with my right hand while simultaneously using his force to toss him toward the floor. The big guy stumbled, then rolled a full circle across the floor before crashing into the back wall near the closet.

More footsteps entered the room. I glanced over my shoulder to see a guard standing near the door with his mouth gaped.

Ivan grunted and growled as he crawled to his feet. "I'll kill you," he yelled, charging me.

He attempted a tackle, but I clutched the front of his shirt while rolling backward to the floor and kicking him up and over me. He soared through the air and slid across the floor. The guard standing by the door sprang out of the way as the big guy crashed into the wall.

Ivan jumped to his feet and punched the wall while glowering at me. I felt annoyed and heat rose in my stomach. I removed one of my knives from my ankle holster and flung it at him. The blade pierced the wall three inches from his face. Ivan's nose crinkled and the white of his eyes grew larger.

"You," he barked while adjusting his stance to rush me for the third time.

The guard jumped in front of Ivan, placed his hands on the big guy's chest, and nudged the angry man against the wall.

"Cálmate. Cálmate," the guard said. "Calm down."

"Get off me," Ivan said, slapping his colleague's hands away.

While the two men shoved and exchanged words, more footsteps approached the door. Another guard entered the room with Navarro behind him.

"What's going on here?" Navarro asked.

Ivan pointed at me. "This guy took our vehicle and left us stranded," he said, still fighting with the guard.

"Oh, is that what happened?" Navarro asked, walking

toward Ivan. "I was informed that you incited the conflict, and Mr. White only finished it."

Ivan looked at Navarro but said nothing.

Navarro yanked my knife from the wall and held it with both hands while fixing upon it as if he admired its design. He then turned from Ivan and walked toward me.

"I'm very interested in how he managed to get the drop on you, my head of security, and two other guards," he said, stopping halfway to me and glancing back at Ivan. "Maybe I should hire him as my head of security."

Ivan lowered his head, and Navarro walked to me. He waved the knife in my face.

"You're pretty good with this, huh?" he said while patting the blade against the palm of his hand. "For someone who's only a fighter. Were you in the military?"

I said nothing.

Navarro pointed the knife at me. "Yeah. I think before your life of crime, you spend some time in the military."

I shrugged. "So?"

"So, it appears you have some skills you weren't forth-coming about?"

"Do you share everything you know and all of your involvements?" I asked.

Ivan exhaled sharply. "Boss, he can't be trusted," he said.

Navarro flung his free hand in the air. A gesture that beck-oned for Ivan to remain silent. Still looking at me, Navarro smiled, his dimples cutting into his cheeks, exposing his straight white teeth. I couldn't stand it. I wanted to punch Mr. GQ in his face but had to play it smart.

"Let me have them," he said.

"Excuse me?"

"The other knives."

"What?"

"You heard him," Ivan said in a demanding tone from across the room.

I looked at him, then knelt and unstrapped the knife holsters, and handed them to Navarro. *Play it smart.*

"Thank you," Navarro said, placing the free knife in its holster before pivoting and handing both holsters to the guard closest to him. "Let's go for a walk."

Navarro exited the door first, and I followed behind him. On my way out, Ivan glared at me.

"If you try to stab me with a knife again—" he grumbled.

"I missed on purpose," I said. "With a head as wide as yours, it'd be impossible to miss if I was trying."

I heard him growl as I left the room and trailed Navarro down the hall. Ivan and the other two guards were last to exit. We all bent the corner at the end of the hall, walked through the living area, then into the dining room. While there, Navarro beckoned the guard, whom he had given my holsters to, with a wave. The man hustled to his boss, and Navarro whispered something in his ear. The guard nodded, glanced at me, then walked into the living room. Navarro opened the same French doors we walked through the day before and we all stepped onto the patio.

Immediately, the sound of rotors chopped through the air. I looked to the backyard and saw a helicopter approaching from the mountains.

Navarro looked at his watch. "Perfect timing," he said. "It appears one of my guests has arrived early."

We walked to the end of the patio and watched as the chopper approached and landed on the helipad at the bottom of the hill in the middle of the field. Two suits exited the helicopter, ducked, and crouch walked toward the walkway leading up the hill as the power from the turbine pulled at their clothes. One of Navarro's guards was waiting to escort them toward the house. As the group of men made their way up the steps, the helicopter rose and veered back in the direction from which it came. I glanced to my right and saw Ivan on the opposite side of the patio, staring at me. His nostrils flared and tension protruded from his jaws. He wanted a piece of me. And I didn't really care. If he wanted another whooping, I'd be happy to give it to him.

After a few minutes, the two men in suits appeared in the backyard. One was taller, with an average frame and a plain beige face. The other wore shades, and I'd seen him before. *Ken the K.O. King*, my opponent. He had the same lean, muscular frame and dark-brown hair that he had in the footage. As the men walked across the grass and past the flowers and shrubs toward us, Navarro met them halfway and shook Ken's hand.

"It's a pleasure to have you here," he said.

Ken nodded but said nothing.

"Your sponsor didn't come with you?" Navarro asked.

"No, just me and my trainer," Ken said.

"Okay, well, I guess he'll be here a little later. My staff will show you to your room," Navarro said before turning to the guard who escorted the men. "Show them to their rooms and make sure they get whatever they need."

"Yes, sir," the guard said.

The men walked past us and Ken glanced at me twice as they did.

"That's him?" he said to his trainer.

His trainer nodded.

"This should be easy money."

Arrogant, I like it, I thought as the men continued down the patio and toward the house. *Makes my job a lot easier.*

"What do you think, Mr. White?" Navarro asked me.

"About what?"

"Your opponent."

"What's there to think?"

"Think it'll be a good fight?"

"Depends—do you think my other fights were good?"

"Yeah, but they ended a little too fast."

"Expect more of the same."

Navarro smirked. "Let's head down to the hangar. I want to show you something."

Me, Navarro, Ivan, and the two guards walked through the backyard and down the steps to the field. As we dodged a few cacti and strode past the helipad, a breeze and sand particles struck my face. Navarro nodded to one of the guards when we arrived at the hangar. The guard returned the nod, then walked to the hangar's door and slid it open. We entered onto a polished concrete floor. Fumes of exhaust and oil immediately hit my nose. Coned pendant lights hung from the high ceilings, and the tank from earlier sat in the center of the hangar.

"This way," Navarro said while pointing his thumb in the tank's direction.

I followed behind him as he circled the tank. Ivan and the two guards trailed at a distance. Once on the other side of the tank, Navarro stopped and faced the north wall. The moment I cleared the corner of the tank, I saw Long sitting on the floor with his head down and his hands tied behind his back, but he wasn't alone. Sitting next to him was Sam.

CHAPTER
SIXTEEN

I QUICKLY TURNED to Navarro. He grinned. As I shifted my sights to Ivan and the two guards, the clacking of aimed guns stuffed the air. The two guards had their submachine guns on me, and Ivan stood with his eyebrows squished together and his lips parted.

Navarro cocked his head and raised his eyebrows. "Did you think I wouldn't find out about you, Mr. White?" he said.

I said nothing. Just looked at him, then at Ivan and the guards.

Ivan nodded with a smile on his face.

"You thought you could get away with it," Navarro continued.

"Get away with what?" I asked.

Navarro chuckled. "Let's not play this game."

"What game?"

"You're going to tell me you know nothing about the girls going missing?"

"Girls?"

"Ramos' wife and daughter."

"What?" Ivan said.

I winced. "They're missing? How?" I asked.

"How did this happen?" Ivan said at the same time.

Navarro walked to Sam. "That's what we're here to find out," he said while eying Sam. He pivoted and looked at Ivan. "If I had to guess, they escaped while my head of security was on a joy ride with my security staff and fighter."

Ivan turned his head and sighed while looking at the floor.

Navarro turned to Sam. "But the janitor was the one who took them breakfast and lunch, so I'm sure he knows something." Navarro knelt and faced Sam. "You remember what happened last time you tried to interfere in my business?" he said while patting Sam's bad leg.

Sam gave Navarro a hard stare. Navarro smirked, then stood and walked to Ivan.

"I'm sure he had help," Navarro continued. "And I think Mr. Long might know something about that," he said, nodding at Long, who still had his head hanging toward the floor.

"What about him?" Ivan said, pointing at me. "I'm sure he's involved with this."

Navarro looked at me through squinted eyes while cuffing his chin. "Did he leave the premise any time before you took him off site?" he asked Ivan.

"I don't think so," Ivan said.

"Do you know if he had any contact with the girls?"

"Not sure?"

"Can you be certain the girls didn't escape while you were on your little ride?"

"No."

"Of course not. You weren't here."

Ivan took in a deep breath, then slowly exhaled. "I learned that Hector guy is involved with the—" he started.

"DEA," Navarro interrupted as he stepped to my face. "And since Mr. White has ties to Hector, he could be with the DEA."

"Yeah," Ivan said.

"Do you work for the DEA?" Navarro asked me.

"I work for myself," I said.

Navarro hunched his shoulders. "See," he said to Ivan. "Maybe he works for the DEA, maybe he doesn't. Either way, he works for me tonight. There's too much money on the table." Navarro looked at Sam and Long. "But we know of at least one person who has connections to the DEA," he continued.

Navarro glanced me over, then waved a guard to me.

"What are you doing?" I asked Navarro as the guard zip-tied my hands behind my back.

He ignored me and threaded through the group before standing next to Ivan. "This is what's going to happen," he said while pointing at me. "You're going to fight for me. If you do well, I may have more work for you. But right now, I'm not sure I can trust you."

"You scum. You're going to pay for this," Sam blurted.

Navarro darted to Sam, knelt, then faced him. "Who's going to make me?" he said in a slow, eerie tone.

"You said I have connections to the DEA," Sam said. "Who's to say they're not on their way here now?"

Navarro crinkled his nose and shook his head while standing. "You've been here for a while and there's been no sign of the DEA. And how would you even know how to get here? You were blind-folded when you arrived and have never left the compound."

Sam smirked.

Noticing the smirk, Navarro winced. "Oh. You think this place is easy to find? That address, you know, it's what we call a phantom address in the criminal world. It's a very elaborate arrangement that insures I get legitimate mail, but it's never, ever delivered directly here. There's no physical location for that address."

Sam's smirked morphed into a frown.

Navarro chuckled and walked toward Ivan. As he did, the guard who zip-tied me guided me to where Sam and Long sat.

"Sit," he said to me.

"I'll stand," I said.

The guard puffed his chest. "I said sit!"

I glared at him.

"Let him stand," Navarro told the guard before turning to Ivan. "Keep them here," he said to the big guy. "But an hour before the fight, bring him to the house to get prepared for his match. Other than that, I don't want them leaving this hangar. Think you can handle that?"

"Yeah," Ivan said with a sigh.

Navarro glanced back at us, his hostages. His eyes scanned from left to right. Hitting Sam, then Long, and stopping on me. I locked eyes with him and, after a moment, he scoffed and walked away toward the hangar's entrance. When he disappeared outside, Ivan strolled to me with a grin on his face. He stood and faced me for a moment without saying a word, but I knew what he was thinking. I saw his right fist clench and dart toward my gut. With my hands tied behind my back, the only thing I could do was tense my abs. His fist slammed into my stomach, and I doubled over and shuffled backward a couple of steps before smacking into the wall that Sam and Long had their backs against. I know I had timed it right, because I didn't feel any pain in my stomach. The force made it look a lot worse than what it actually was. Either way, I was mad. When I lifted my head, I fixed on Ivan. *The next time we dance, you won't walk away from it,* I thought.

"I'll see you soon, Mr. Fighter," Ivan said to me before gesturing for the guards to follow him toward the front of the hangar. "Let's go," he continued. "I want this hangar locked down. One of you outside in the front, and the other at the back."

A moment after that, they exited the hangar, and the door rattled, then slammed shut.

"This isn't good," Sam said.

"Nope. I bet you wished you left now," I told him before looking at Long.

Sam noticed. "He was here when they brought me," he said. "Had his head down the whole time."

"Yeah. He saw his friend blown to pieces by a tank. That's a lot to take in."

"Oh."

I tapped Long's leg with my foot. "Long," I said.

He grunted but kept his head down.

"Long, time to snap out of it. We have to work together if we wanna make it out alive."

Long shook his head. "What for?" he muttered. "We're already dead."

"He speaks," I said. "But obviously for himself 'cause I feel very much alive."

Long looked up at me. "No. We're all gonna die here, and no one will know or care," he said before dropping his head again.

I looked at Sam, and he glanced at me while gently shaking his head. I guess he wanted me to back off Long, but I didn't see it that way.

"So, just like that, you're giving up?" I said to Long. "I'm sure you have someone that's counting on you to fight. Maybe a parent or close friend or sister."

Long looked at me when I said *sister*.

"Whatta ya suggest we do, huh?" he said.

"Let's start with intelligence gathering?"

"What?"

"How'd you get into this situation?"

Long turned his head away and sighed.

"Well, allow me to take a stab," I said. "When you were younger, you had a few run-ins with the law, but nothing too elaborate. And in your adult years you were on the straight, but about three months ago you ran into some financial troubles and started hanging with people in low places again. That's when you met Snyder."

Long looked at me but said nothing.

I nodded. "Yeah."

Long exhaled sharply. "There's more to it than that. I have a sister I have to look after and protect. She's the sweetest person, and I don't won't anything to happen to her. I'm afraid if I make the wrong move now, Navarro will go after her."

"I met your sister, Kelly. She is a kind person."

Long eyes widened. "What? When?"

"It doesn't matter. What I'm unclear on is if the FBI approached you before, or after you started working for Navarro."

"You're with the FBI?" Sam asked Long.

The spiky blond shook his head. "Not with them," he said. "I'm an informant. The FBI has been investigating Navarro for months, so they had eyes on Snyder, which means they had eyes on me. I guess they determined I had the most to lose, so after a month of working for Navarro, they approached me. They threatened to charge me and look into my past for other crimes they could stack onto the charges. Even threatened to investigate my sister until they found something."

Sam shook his head. "That's terrible," he said.

"It is. Sometimes the American government plays dirty," I said. "But if you play with fire, expect to get burnt."

Long nodded gravely. "I know. And now Navarro suspects that I'm an informant."

"I used to work for the DEA," Sam blurted before looking at me.

The comment didn't shock or surprise me, so my demeanor remained neutral.

"I've been investigating the Escarra cartel for about five and a half years," Sam continued. "And about four years ago, while following up on a lead near Nye, I was ambushed. I didn't anticipate any trouble, so I didn't ask my partner to come with me, but Navarro and his team got the drop on me. The little punk was feeling himself and shot me in the leg. He'd just taken over the business from his father, so was probably on some type of power trip."

"Where's his father now?" I asked.

"He passed a couple of years back," Sam said. "But anyway, they blindfolded me, then brought me here. Took their time getting me medical attention, and I've been here ever since as their janitor." Sam inhaled, then struggled to swallow. "Away from my family. My friends. My work. My life. Imma make that sleazebag pay."

"You'll get your chance," I said before walking toward the center of the hangar.

When I cleared just beyond the army tank, I walked to a bench near the wall to my right and scanned the top of it for anything that could help me get out of my restraints. The bench-top was empty, so I found nothing of use. I walked back to where Sam and Long sat.

"What are you doing?" Sam asked.

"Looking for something to help me get out of these thick zip-ties," I said.

"Any luck?"

"Not yet."

I walked to the back wall and searched the floor for anything I could use. When I reached the middle of the wall, there was a portion of drywall missing, exposing the studs. One stud had a long screw protruding from the side of it. I turned my back to the wall and angled the adjoining section of the zip-tie on the screw, then raked it across the screw's threads. Back and forward, back and forward. This went on for nearly two minutes before I felt the zip-tie give some. As I pivoted from the wall and widened my stance, a faint whoop-ing-chopping sound approached from the northwest. In an attempt to break my restraints, I pulled my arms apart and after five seconds of straining, the zip-tie popped and a rapid shock raced from my wrists up to my shoulders. The whooping and chopping drew closer as I removed the zip-tie debris from my wrists and walked toward Sam and Long. When I was halfway to them, I heard three faint but distinct pops. Much more boisterous than a zip-tie breaking. It was gunfire.

CHAPTER
SEVENTEEN

AS I APPROACHED Sam and Long, more shots rang from the mansion.

"What's that noise?" Sam asked.

"Which one? The helicopter or the gunfire?" I said, while searching the area where they sat.

"Get us out of here," Long said.

"That's what I'm trying to do."

Before I could complete that sentence, rattling and voices flowed from the hangar's door. I turned to face the door and saw a strip of light enter as the door slid open.

"What's happening?" Sam asked.

Long said nothing, but his squinted eyes and gaped mouth asked me the same question.

"They're coming in—we'll have to wait," I said before sitting on the floor next to Long and placing my hands behind my back.

The door continued to roll and bounce open and the sounds from the gunfire and helicopter rotors grew louder. Shortly after, footsteps rushed across the floor and four guards raced to our position. Two immediately hopped on the hull of the M25 tank while the other two stood and looked at us.

A muscular guard on top of the hull looked down at the other two guards.

"What are you doing?" he said with a shrug.

The skinnier of the two guards standing on the floor nodded at us. "What about them?" he asked.

"One of you stay with them, but we'll need the other to help take down this chopper. Ahora."

Sam and I looked at each other.

"Alright," the skinny guard said before whispering something to his heavier partner, then climbing onto the hull of the tank.

A moment later, the muscular guard along with the guard he hopped up with originally climbed onto the turret, opened its hatch, and then disappeared inside while the skinny guard opened the driver's hatch near the front of the tank.

The bulky guard on the floor with us kept his hands on his submachine gun and repeatedly shared his gaze between the tank and us.

"What's going on?" I asked him.

"Shut up," he said before gesturing for us to stand.

Long and I immediately stood, but it took Sam ten seconds longer to get to his feet. I kept my wrists hidden behind my back as the guard directed us further along the wall and away from the tank.

"Sit," the bulky guard said. "And don't move," he continued as we followed his instructions.

I kept my eyes on the tank. The skinny guard eased down the hatch, and seconds later, the twin V8 engines at the back came to life. His head poked through the driver's hatch, the wheels rotated, and the caterpillar tracks turned. The bulky guard on the floor with us watched as the tank rolled toward the front of the hangar. When it was close to the center, I sprung from the floor and rushed him. The hefty man attempted to raise his gun at me, but I was already on him. I pushed the machine gun into his gut with one hand while spearing him in the throat with my free hand. The gun dropped to the man's side, and he reached for his throat. As he did, I slid one of my legs behind him, then tossed him over and onto the floor. His back hit the ground, and he coughed a rigid breath before I stomped his face and put him to sleep. As he lay on the floor, I removed the submachine gun from him and patted him down. I found a Beretta 9mm, two spare magazines for it, and a knife on his person. I quickly stuffed the Beretta into the back of my pants and slipped the spare magazines into my front pocket. On my way to Sam and Long, I draped the machine gun over my shoulder and readied the knife.

The gunfire from the mansion continued while the noise from the helicopter whirling toward us increased. I cut Sam's zip-tie first, then Long's. As the two men stood, I handed Sam the machine gun.

"I'm sure you know how to use this," I said to him while pivoting toward the front of the hangar.

"Looks like the calvary made it after all," he said.

"Calvary?" Long said

"Yeah," I said, skip-stepping in preparation to sprint after the tank, which was close to the hangar door.

"Where ya going?" Sam called after me.

"To stop the tank," I yelled back. "If they take out the chopper, this won't end well."

"How on earth are you gonna do that?"

"Just stay alive. I got this," I said before dashing after the tank.

I caught up with the heavy piece of machinery just as it was exiting the hangar. As the tank's tracks created clouds of dust, I clenched the tank's side skirt and heaved myself up and onto the hull. The sun hit my eyes, and the helicopter rotors chopping through the air rang my ears. I shielded my eyes while looking at the sky and saw a black helicopter approaching from about three hundred yards out. More gunfire from the mansion barked over the grinding of the tank. I looked through the dust cloud and didn't see much activity from the house's backyard or patio, so I figured all the action must be coming from the front. When I turned to look at the helicopter, the tank's turret spun. Once the main gun was horizontally in line with the aircraft, the gun raised vertically and the tank slowed. I balanced myself and crouch walked to the front of the tank. The skinny guard still had his head poking out the driver's hatch. It took me seconds to reach him, and when I did, the tank stopped moving completely.

"Hey," I called to him.

The guard turned his head toward me, and my shoe met his face. His head hit the hatch's side and he immediately took a nap. I grabbed him underneath his armpits and lifted him from the driver's compartment and onto the hull. The helicopter was very close and the tank's turret was still moving ever so slightly, no doubt adjusting its aim. I slid down the driver's hatch and into the driver's seat of the cleanest tank I'd ever seen. In all my years in the army, no vehicle came close to how immaculate this tank's interior looked and smelled. Realizing I only had seconds before the tank was ready to fire at the helicopter, I located the turret traversing door which led from the driver's compartment to the turret basket, then quickly released the hand brakes, pressed the neutral pedal, then threw the lever into drive to move the tank off target and buy myself some time.

"Hey, why'd you move?" the voice of the muscular guard said from inside the turret basket.

After pulling the hand brakes into park, I looked around and found a fire extinguisher behind the driver's seat. I picked it up, pulled the pin, opened the turret traversing door, then sprayed inside the turret basket.

I heard the two guards inside yelling and coughing. I quickly pulled myself through the driver's hatch and outside onto the hull. The turret hatch opened and fire extinguisher smoke puffed from inside the turret as the muscular guard climbed from the hatch, sneezing and hacking. He tripped as he exited the hatch and fell over to the opposite side of the tank. The other guard exited and rolled over on his back on the top of the turret. He coughed, then rolled his head back and looked at me. His eyes widened, and he leaned forward, reaching for his sidearm. I darted to him, and he swung his right arm in my direction with his Beretta clenched. I grabbed his arm and slammed it against the top of the turret. The gun fell and clanked on the hull before spinning off the tank toward the dirt. I pushed the man's chin back until he lay straight on the turret, then axed my elbow between his chest and throat. As he reached for his throat and hugged his chest, I knocked him out with a right cross.

I jumped from the tank, and the moment my feet hit the ground, I heard footsteps shuffle toward me. When I turned, I saw the muscular guard charging toward me. His eyes were watery and dirt covered his hair and clothes. He swung at me wildly. I ducked under the punch and planted my right heel into the groove behind his right knee. The guard knelt, but quickly swung at me with a back fist. I stepped back as he turned to me and crawled to his feet. Before he could completely stand, I kicked him in the groin and he doubled over. I then clenched the back of his head with both my hands and delivered a thunderous knee to his face. The big guy's head jerked, and he tumbled backward into the dirt.

My clothes pulled from my body, and sand spiraled near me. My gaze moved toward the sky, and I saw the helicopter descending toward the helipad. On my way to the steps leading up to the backyard patio, I saw Sam and Long exiting the hangar. Sam waved as the wind from the helicopter pulled at his clothes. I waved back, then raced up the steps.

Just before reaching the backyard, I glanced down at the field and saw five armed personnel exiting the helicopter, all dressed in black tactical gear with helmets and armed with assault rifles. I squinted and made out the letters FBI written on one of their vests. Wasn't sure how they found us but was happy they did. I turned my attention to the mansion and continued into the backyard and onto the patio.

We have some unfinished business, Navarro. I'm coming.

When I made it a few yards from the mansion, the French doors leading into the dining room opened and two armed guards exited with their machine guns drawn. I darted to my left and dove behind a brick fireplace near the hot tub and pool. Bullets whizzed by and chunks of concrete splintered and chipped from the fireplace as I ducked behind it and removed the Beretta from my back waistband. Booms continued to stuff the air and debris flung on me. I waited for it. That moment of silence. That brief window of opportunity that I'd exploited so many times before. It came. The gunfire ceased, and I quickly leaned from behind the fireplace, aimed at the guard closest to me, and pulled the trigger twice before immediately swinging my aim to the other guard and pulling the trigger twice more. Both center mass shots. Both men dropped to the pavement. I walked to the first guard and kicked his gun away from him and did the same with the second before entering through the French doors and into the dining area.

The room was empty. With the Beretta trained in front of me, I continued toward the living area, and just as I entered the living room, more gunfire came from the foyer. I cleared the living room and crept toward the foyer. Two of Navarro's guards lay on the floor between the grand staircase. As I scanned their bodies, footsteps knocked on the floor. My gaze lifted and two men dressed in full tactical gear, like the individuals I saw exit the helicopter, approached me with their rifles aimed.

"Drop it!" one of them said.

"Hands up!" the other said.

I don't know why, but I found it shocking that even at the federal level, some law enforcement didn't understand how barking conflicting commands could be confusing.

I lowered my gun and placed my free hand between myself and them. "Friendly," I said.

"Black," I heard a familiar but labored voice say. "He's with us."

I peered around the men and saw Jessica. She had her caramel hair tied into a knot and wore a bullet-proof vest with DEA on it. She was sweaty, with streaks of grime smeared on her face and arms.

"He's our asset," she continued, nearly out of breath.

"Jessica?" I said.

The two FBI agents lowered their guns, and I walked past them to Jessica. Before either of us could say anything, another familiar voice came from upstairs.

"Freeze!" Deidra yelled.

I trained my gun ahead as I walked into the foyer.

"You two secure the first floor," I heard Jessica instructing the FBI agents. "We'll go upstairs."

I looked up the stairwell to my right and saw Deidra making her way up the steps while peering through the sights of an assault rifle. As Jessica approached me and brought her rifle to bear, I glanced around the foyer and saw two more of Navarro's men sprawled on the floor.

"I'll cover you," Jessica said to me.

I nodded at her before pointing my 9mm Beretta at the stairs and making my way up the steps. By the time we reached the second floor, Deidra had disappeared down the east wing hall. Two loud blasts clapped from the hall.

"Stop! Freeze!" Deidra yelled again.

When Jessica and I entered the hall, a door at the end of the hallway smacked into the wall, and I saw Deidra's back as she ran inside. We hurried toward the room, stepping over the body of one of Navarro's guards as we did. On the other side of the doorway, a spacious library greeted us. Bookshelves surrounded us on either side. And on the opposite end of the room, a spiral framed metal staircase led up to a second level with more bookshelves. Deidra chased Navarro in that direction.

I stopped, lowered my gun, and quickly surveyed the situation while Jessica ran past me.

"C'mon, Black," she beckoned.

To my right, I caught movement in my peripheral. One of the book shelves teetered, then toppled over directly in line with Jessica's position.

"Watch out!" I shouted.

CHAPTER
EIGHTEEN

JESSICA FROZE AND watched as the bookshelf plunged toward her. She stuttered in her steps conflicted about which direction to move. She shuffled to her left, but the bookshelf hit her right shoulder and pushed her toward the wooden shelves on the opposite side. Her head smacked against the wood and she collapsed to the floor.

"Jessica!" I said before looking toward the opposite end of the fallen shelf and seeing Ken's trainer standing where the shelf once had.

As I lifted my pistol to target him, something slapped my right hand. I looked down and saw the gun fall from my hands along with a shiny, black Crockett & Jones dress shoe coming toward my face. I tilted my head back while hopping backward simultaneously, barely dodging the foot. As my head nodded forward, I widened my stance and raised my fist at the owner of the foot. It was Ken. He had on the same suit as earlier and murderous intensity on his face as he stepped into a fighting stance and glared at me. As he and I squared off, I scanned the room. Jessica lay on the floor moaning with her hand pressed against the side of her head. Ken's trainer looked toward the far end of the room where

Deidra chased Navarro up the spiral staircase before swinging his gaze in mine and Ken's direction. The trainer sprinted toward us, stopped beside Ken, then slid into a fighting stance.

Ken made the first move. He skip-stepped toward me with a front kick, but I stepped outside the attack while parrying his leg and pushing his shoulder in one motion. He stumbled forward a few steps while his trainer rushed me with a right cross. I bobbed under the punch and delivered an uppercut to his chin while slipping to his right side. The trainer shuffled backward, and I pressed after him with three quick jabs. A right to the chest, a left to the mouth, then another right to the chest. He slammed into a bookshelf. I caught him with another uppercut to the chin, but this one had a lot more force. The trainer's head jerked backward before nodding forward as his body slumped to the floor. I danced backward to recollect myself but had little time as Ken was soaring toward me with a flying kick.

Having just a second to react, I raised my forearms together above my head and absorbed the attack. The impact forced my arms apart and sent me shuffling backward. I lifted my foot behind me and kicked off a bookshelf to break my momentum before easing into a fighting stance. After glancing at his trainer sprawled on the floor, Ken glared at me, raised his fist, then inched toward me. When he was three feet away, he feinted a punch and threw a low roundhouse kick. I lifted my leg and blocked his kick. He followed his attack with a cross. I parried the punch while simultaneously jabbing him in the gut, then hip tossing him to the floor. Ken quickly jumped to his feet.

"You," he growled before rushing me.

As he thrust a sidekick at me, I stepped back and slapped his foot away. He continued his assault with two jabs. I blocked both, then ducked just in time to dodge the round-house he launched at my head. As the breeze from my opponent's kick swept over my head, I slid in and hit him in his ribs with a left hook followed by a right hook to his gut. Ken bowed forward and stumbled backward. I followed him and delivered a solid front kick to his solar plexus. He flopped backward, then smacked into a bookshelf.

"You're not new to fighting," he said between pants.

"Never said I was," I replied. "Now give it up."

Ken wiped the slobber from his mouth with the back of his hand. "I don't think so," he said while shaking his head and easing back into a fighting stance.

We stared at each other for three seconds before he charged at me with two wild jabs. I parried both, and he continued with a kick, which I evaded. I knew what he was attempting to do. And after blocking another one of his kicks and jab, I waited. Ken shifted his stance before jumping in the air. He was performing the same flying knee attack I saw him do in his highlight reel. Expecting the attack, I stepped closer while he was in mid-air and snatched his leg before he could fully extend his knee. He smacked the floor face first before palming his face with both hands and rolling onto his back. I walked to him, knelt, then put him to sleep with a punch to the forehead. I heard moans and turned to find Jessica squirming on the floor. She leaned forward, and I jogged to her and helped her to her feet. She palmed the side of her head and groaned.

"What'd I miss?" she said before arching toward her rifle on the floor.

"Hold on," I said while grabbing her shoulders and standing her upright. "Take it easy," I continued before bending down, picking up the rifle, and handing it to her.

"Thanks," she said.

"Give yourself a moment to find your footing."

A loud blast echoed across the library. Both Jessica and I looked toward the second level.

"You should—" Jessica started.

"On it. You rest here a minute," I said, while dodging the fallen bookshelf and racing toward the spiral staircase on the opposite side of the library. It took me less than five seconds to make it to the second level.

"You're gonna pay!" Deidra yelled.

I turned at the corner to my left and rushed across the walkway, toward her voice. At midpoint of the walkway was an open door leading outside to a large, half-circle balcony. Deidra stood panting with her rifle trained in front of her. On the other side of her gun, Navarro knelt on both knees and held his right shoulder while blood seeped through the cracks of his fingers. His mouth and eyes were both wide open.

"What? Wait—" he said.

"No, you killed him and now you're going to die."

Navarro's eyebrows knitted. "Killed who? What are you—"

"Shut up," Deidra demanded.

It didn't look good for Navarro, and I felt tempted to let the situation play out, but I knew he didn't do what she thought he did.

"Deidra," I said.

"Stay out of this, Black," she said, maintaining her focus on Navarro.

Navarro squinted and gently shook his head while mouthing the word, *Black*.

"Look, I know this guy deserves to be buried," I said. "But I don't believe he did what you think he did. And he has a lot of information you can use to put him and a lot of other criminals under the jail."

Deidra shook her head. "No, he did it. And I don't want to give him the chance to use his connections to weasel his way out," she said, taking a step toward Navarro.

"Please don't. I beg you," Navarro said.

My eyebrows rose. *He's definitely a beggar.* "Wait," I said to Deidra. "I know he's a weasel who'll go back to his old ways when he feels his neck is no longer on the line. But I'm telling you, for guys like him, there are things worse than death. And how would you feel if you killed him, and he didn't do what you thought he did?"

"I'd sleep like a babe," she said.

I shrugged. "Okay, I can see that."

"What do you mean he didn't do what I thought he did?" she asked me.

I walked to her. "I think we should cuff this piece of trash," I said while removing her handcuffs from the holster on her back waistband. "Then go downstairs and see."

For the first time, she glanced at me. I forced a smile before walking to Navarro, lifting him from the floor, and slapping the cuffs around his wrists.

"You said you didn't work for the DEA," he said.

"I don't."

"Are you even a real fighter?"

"Ask Ken. When he wakes up," I said before pushing him toward the door. "Move it."

I walked him into the library and down the spiral staircase with Deidra trailing behind a few paces. We stepped over the fallen bookshelf and approached Jessica.

"You okay?" she asked Deidra.

"I'm fine. Are you okay?"

"Yeah. I had a bit of a fall, but I'm okay now."

Deidra nodded.

Two armed FBI agents entered the library with their guns aimed. When they realized the situation was under control, they lowered their weapons.

"These two," Jessica said while pointing to the floor at Ken, then at his trainer.

As the agents walked to the men, Deidra pointed at Navarro.

"Him too," she said while looking the criminal up and down.

I shoved Navarro to Jessica. She caught him, and a minute later, she and the two agents exited the library with Navarro, Ken, and the trainer.

Deidra leaned against a bookshelf, then tilted her head back and exhaled. "This has been a long day," she said.

"Tell me about it," I said. "This case is pretty personal, huh?"

Deidra looked at me as she stood straight and sighed. "Yeah. Black, listen, I'm—I'm sorry. That scumbag di—" she started.

I interrupted her with a hand gesture. "Don't worry about apologizing," I said. "Just know I'm finished, and I don't want to hear anything about charges or giving a statement."

Deidra nodded and huffed a chuckle. "Okay," she said.

"How did you find this place? Navarro mentioned it was a phantom address."

"The license plate number you left in the drop box."

"Oh, yeah—the Cayenne Snyder and Long were driving."

"Yep. Had to call in a few favors, but after using traffic cameras and satellite imagery, we were able to track them here."

I nodded.

Deidra stared at me with pursed lips, and after a moment, she adjusted the rifle strap over her shoulder and stepped closer to me. "I'm happy you're okay. And thank you."

"Like I said, I don't want to—" I started before seeing the sincerity in her eyes. "Don't mention it. I'm sure you would've caught Navarro eventually."

"That's not what I meant," she said. "I was gonna kill him in cold blood."

I glanced at the floor. "Don't be so hard on yourself," I said. "I'm sure there's a long line of people who want to kill Navarro. Me included."

Deidra shook her head. "No, this is different. It felt like

something was taking over me. You don't understand what he did."

"I told you, he didn't do it."

She looked at me and squinted. "So, he didn't?"

"No. That's what I was trying to tell you."

"I thought you were just saying that to stop me from shooting him."

I winced. "Yeah, like I care about him that much."

"Wait. What do you think he did—are you sure?"

I smiled. "Go downstairs and see for yourself."

Her eyes widened, and she cuffed her mouth with her hands before hitting me on my shoulder and rushing out the library. I followed her through the hall and past a few FBI agents on our way to the main staircase. We zipped downstairs to the foyer where Jessica stood with the two FBI agents who were in the library earlier. Walking from between the double staircase and toward the foyer were Sam and Long. They were both handcuffed, with FBI agents walking next to them.

"You can uncuff him," I said to the FBI agent walking with Sam.

The agent removed a key and worked on Sam's cuffs. Deidra's forehead and eyebrows furrowed as her mouth gaped. When the cuffs were off Sam, he rubbed his wrist and looked to the foyer.

"Thanks," he said to me before locking eyes with Deidra.

The two stared at each other for a few moments before slowly closing the eighteen foot gap between them.

"Baby girl," Sam said with a quiver in his voice when they were five feet away.

"Dad," Deidra said as the two closed the gap and embraced each other.

I turned to Jessica, and she shook her head and squinted at the sight of Deidra and Sam. While the group watched the father and daughter reunite, I slipped out the foyer and down the hall to Navarro's office. I circled his desk and opened the drawer. I found my knife holsters and the cell phone I had received from the DEA. After placing my property in their respective places on my person, I walked back into the foyer and stepped next to Jessica. Deidra and Sam held each other's hand. They exchanged some whispers, then embraced again.

"They're still at it?" I said.

"I'm still in shock," Jessica said. "I'm sure she told me her father had died."

I cocked my head. "Well, looks like she was mistaken," I said before scanning around the house, now crawling with armed agents. "Where's Vargas? He's sitting this one out?"

Jessica pivoted to me. "We couldn't get him to sit this out," she said. "He's raiding Ramos' house with a separate FBI unit."

"Oh, speaking of which, Ramos' wife and daughter—"

"The FBI picked them up after the wife called Deidra."

"Good," I said.

"They're gonna be disappointed when they go home and find Ramos is arrested. Especially that little girl."

"Yeah."

"I hate seeing kids suffer," she said, pivoting back in Deidra's and Sam's direction. "Vargas is definitely taking time off once this is over. Even if I have to make him."

"What do you mean?"

Jessica looked at me. "Oh, you don't know?" she said.

"Know what?"

"Vargas's son has a... medical condition. It can become dangerous but is very treatable. Just expensive. He's been a bit stressed about it, but we're all gonna chip in to see what we can do. There's plenty of time for treatment, but I can imagine for a parent it feels like torture knowing your kid has an illness."

"Oh, makes sense."

"What?"

"Nothing—you think he's still at Ramos'?" I asked her.

"Yeah, probably."

"Can you call him? I wanna talk to him."

Jessica's eyebrows knitted. "Sure," she said, removing her phone and tapping at the screen. "But don't tell him I told you, since he didn't tell you himself."

"I won't."

She handed me the phone as it was calling. I walked away toward the front door and held the phone to my ear, nearly bumping into a passing EMT as I did. After a few rings, Vargas' voice came onto the line.

"Agent Vargas," he said.

"Vargas."

"Hi, Black. I was worried about you."

"I'm good here. How about you?"

"Hanging in there. We're wrapping things up at Ramos' house."

"So I heard, but shouldn't you be home?"

The line went silent for a moment.

Vargas sighed into the phone. "Trust me. When we're finished with this case, I'm taking a lot of time off."

"I hear that. Listen, I left a bag of clothes at Ramos' house."

"Okay, you want me to get em' for you?"

"Please. There in the guest house in the room down the short hall. Should be in the bottom dresser drawer under some bed linen."

"Alright."

"I only want the clothes," I said.

"Huh?"

"There's *something* inside the bag for you—just bring me the clothes."

The line went silent again.

"Okay. I got it," Vargas said after a moment.

"Good. Thanks."

"Later."

After ending the call, I walked back to Jessica and handed her the phone.

"Thanks," I said.

"Anytime," she said.

Deidra and Sam finally separated, and an EMT took Sam toward the living area while Deidra approached Jessica and I.

She smiled at me. "How did you know who he was?" she asked.

"I've unraveled much more complex situations, but it's easy to see he's your father."

"Yeah, but how?" Deidra said with a slight chuckle.

"There were a few factors, but two really stuck out to me. First, he acts and talks like a cop. Second, he really admired my haircut."

"What?"

"Yeah, really, Black?" Jessica added.

"It's a long story."

"Anyway," Deidra said. "Thank you for looking out for him."

I shrugged.

"I'm happy you came alone. Not only were you my only hand, but you were my best bet."

"Okay, this is getting too mushy for me," I said while handing Deidra the undercover flip phone. "I'm ready to get back to my life—who's my ride?"

Both Deidra and Jessica laughed.

"Give us a little time to wrap up here," Deidra said. "Then we'll be on our way."

CHAPTER
NINETEEN

IT TOOK THIRTY minutes to wrap up at Navarro's compound and another five and a half hours to make it back to DEA headquarters. A starry night sky accompanied us most of the trip as Deidra, Jessica, Sam, and I all rode in an unmarked SUV with two FBI agents. When we found a parking spot, we crowded out of the car. I walked to my Viper, circled the car, then rejoined the group. We all entered the elevator and rode to the fifth floor. Once there, Jessica took the two FBI agents to the break room while Deidra, Sam, and I went to the team's office. Inside, waiting at Deidra's desk, sat Anson. As we entered, he stood.

"Is that…" he said with his silver eyebrows furrowed.

"Yeah, Will," Sam said with a smile as he made his way to Anson. "It's me."

"My partner," Anson said before the two embraced. "I never lost hope."

The two nudged away from each other, then glanced over one another.

"Look at you," Sam said.

"Look at me. Look at you," Anson said while rubbing his hand across Sam's afro. "Doesn't look like you had a decent haircut since the last time I cut it." He threw his arm around his partner's neck. "We're gonna fix that right now."

The two men chit-chatted and laughed while patting each other on the back as they exited the office.

Deidra smiled at the sight of them.

"They're pretty close, huh?" I said to her.

"Like brothers," she said before circling her desk and opening a drawer. "Here you go." She extended my car keys.

I grabbed them and settled them inside my pocket.

"And as promised," she continued. "Not a single scratch on your car."

"I noticed," I said.

"Well, I guess this is it, Mr—" Deidra started before her phone vibrated. "One sec," she said, holding her index finger to me while removing her cellphone and placing it to her ear. "Agent Harris," she said into the phone. "Oh, he's already here? Really?" She listened into the phone for a few moments before her eyes tilted up to me. "Why does he want to speak with him? I'm not leaving them alone in a room together." She listened a little more before sighing. "No, I'll go in with them. Is Long here too? … Okay. Sure, on my way."

"What was that about?" I asked.

"Navarro is here—in the same interrogation room we had you in. He wants to talk with Long."

I shrugged. "His final request before he goes away for good?" I said.

"Not sure, but it's weird."

I pursed my lips and nodded. "It is."

"But anyhow. It's not for you to worry about," she said while extending her hand. "You're free to g–"

"If you don't mind," I interrupted. "I want to hang out for a little while. Witness Navarro's last request."

The truth be told, Navarro requesting Long's presence interested me.

Deidra smiled. "Follow me," she said.

I followed her out the office and down the hall. We passed the main cubicle area on our way to the interrogation room. Deidra swiped her badge at a panel for the door next to the interrogation room's door. The door clicked opened, and we entered the observation room. Inside stood Jessica, and next to her stood a short man in a suit sporting a magnum mustache, with an FBI badge draped from his neck. The suit eyed Deidra and me as we entered but said nothing.

"This is agent Farlow," Deidra said. "He's Long's FBI contact."

He and I exchanged nods, then I turned to face the observation glass. Navarro sat in the room at the table alone with his right arm in a sling. A strap around his waist confined him to the chair, and they'd shackled his ankles. After a few moments, he looked at the mirror and smirked.

"Cocky bastard, isn't he?" Farlow said.

"You have no idea," Deidra said under her breath.

A knock flowed from the observation room's door. Deidra opened it, and an agent with a handcuffed Long stood on the other side.

"Let's do it," she said, exiting the room into the hall with them.

I glanced at Jessica and Farlow as the two stepped closer to the observation glass. A few moments later, the interrogation room door opened and Navarro adjusted in his seat as it did.

Long entered first, with Deidra a few paces behind him. The door shut, and the two sat in the chairs across from Navarro.

Navarro showed a crooked grin. "Agent Harris," his voice flowed from the speakers inside the observation room. "I wasn't expecting you, but it's good to see you."

"Can't say it's good to see you," Deidra said. "How's your shoulder?"

Navarro's grin turned straight, and he touched his injured

shoulder. "It'll heal," he said. "How does it feel to have your father back?"

"Watch what you say."

Jessica shook her head. "Maybe it's not a good idea to have her in there," she said to Farlow and me.

"Give her some time," Farlow said.

"Just trying to make conversation," Navarro said to Deidra, a smirk arching on his face.

Deidra glared at him. "You sure have a lot to say for a man who was begging for his life earlier today."

Again, Navarro's smirk went straight, and he stared at Deidra.

"Now stop wasting our time and tell us what you want," she continued.

Navarro rolled his eyes away from Deidra and turned to Long. "I just wanted to ask Mr. Long a question," he said.

Long stared at Navarro for a moment before glancing at the tabletop.

"Remember what I did to your friend, Snyder?"

"Threatening a federal informant won't do any good," Deidra said.

"Not threatening him. Just letting him know I'm going to keep my promise."

I thought for a second, then turned to Farlow. "Did you guys arrest Ivan?" I said, before nodding at the window. "His head of security."

Farlow squinted. "Ivan, Ivan, Ivan," he said before widening his eyes as if he realized something. "Navarro's general." He shook his head. "I don't recall seeing him."

"There's not a lot you can do to him from where you're sitting," Deidra said to Navarro.

A smirk crept onto Navarro's face.

"Great," I said, while pivoting toward the door.

"Who said I was going to do anything, and to him?" Navarro said to Deidra.

On my way out the door, I heard Long say, "My sister! You piece of trash!"

As I headed for the elevator, I heard Jessica call, "Black! Where ya going?"

"Kelly Long," I said, pressing the down arrow on the elevator. "She works at the diner up the street from the safe house—motel I stayed in. Send some people there."

The elevator dinged, and the doors thumped open.

"What are you going to do?"

"Try to keep her safe," I said, entering the elevator.

It took me less than two minutes to reach the garage, and another minute to enter my Viper and fire up the engine. I sped out of the garage before shooting past the guard hut and veering onto the road. I drove for nearly a minute before flicking my headlights on. After another seventeen minutes of driving, I slowed as I passed the motel safe house and approached the diner. I skidded into the gravel driveway and sprang from the car with the engine running. When I made it to the front door, I remembered something and was certain I wouldn't find Kelly inside, but I figured I'd check, anyway. Inside sat a few customers and a short, dark-haired waitress served them. I walked through the swinging door and into the kitchen where the heavy-set cook and another cook stood at the grill.

"Can I help you?" the heavy cook asked.

I ignored him and scanned the kitchen, then turned, walked out, and exited the diner. As I was entering my car, I saw the cook open the front door and watch as I sped out of the parking lot and onto the road. It took me just over thirty seconds to make it to the mall. I circled the mall until I reached the parking area nearest the shoe store where Kelly worked. I cruised a few units past and parked at a toy store. After scanning the area, I exited my car and walked across the parking lot, passing a couple of flickering light poles on my way to the shoe store's entrance. The door was locked, but I heard noises coming from an alleyway near the side of the unit.

As I crept toward the alley, two faint, distinct voices struck my ears. One was very familiar. I entered the alley and saw Kelly and her young, thin, pale, dark-haired co-worker entering a side door. The door slowly closed behind them. I dashed to the door and grabbed it before it shut. Stepping into a dark hallway, I closed the door behind myself and saw Kelly and the young man had already made it halfway to the mall's main concourse. Unseen, I followed them as they talked and laughed, then made a left at the concourse. I increased my pace and caught up with them just as they entered the shoe store.

"Hey—what's going—who are you?" the young man said at the sight of me.

Kelly squinted. "Mr. White?" she said.

"You should come with me," I told her.

"What? Why?"

"It's about your brother, Ethan. We have to go."

"How do you know Ethan?"

"It's a long story, but you're in danger and we have to go now."

"I'm calling the cops," the young man said.

I glanced at him. "You do that," I said, before turning to Kelly. "Trust me." The young guy raced inside the shoe store while Kelly stared at me.

"I'm so confused," she said.

"I'll explain on the way," I said, while grabbing her arm and leading her toward the hall.

"You're scaring me. Let me go," she said, snatching her arm away and running down the hall toward the exit.

I chased after her, but she made it outside before I reached her. Removing a knife from my ankle holster, I wedged the door open and followed her outside into the alleyway. Kelly had stopped at the end of the alley just before reaching the parking lot, and as I ran toward her, I saw why she had stopped. Headlights glared at us and tires screeched as a dark sedan jerked to a stop ten yards away. From the back passenger's side door, one of Navarro's guards exited with a submachine gun in hand. Ivan stepped from the front passenger side with a silver pistol in his hand. He stared at me for a moment before gritting his teeth and bringing his gun to bear.

Grabbing Kelly's arm, I pulled her into the alleyway. As we raced toward the door, multiple booms roared behind us, and the surrounding walls splintered and chipped. Once at the door, I yanked it opened and pushed Kelly in before darting inside myself, removing my knife from the door wedge, and shutting the door closed. We raced down the hall as banging and loud voices flowed from the door. Kelly was a few steps ahead of me, so I followed her into the shoe store.

"This won't work," I said. "We have to get you out of here."

"Were those gunshots?" the young man near the counter asked.

"Yea-yeah," Kelly answered while trembling.

"Let's go," I said. "They'll know you're here."

Kelly gently shook her head.

"The..." the young guy said, looking around. "The cops are on their way."

I shook my head. "They won't get here in—" I started before a crash rang from the front of the store.

One of the guards shot out the glass from the front door and burst into the store. As he stumbled inside, he raised his machine gun at us.

CHAPTER
TWENTY

BEFORE HE COULD steady his aim, I flung my knife at him. It pierced the guard's shoulder, and he spun toward his hurt shoulder, firing a few rounds into the ceiling before falling to the floor. As he rolled to his side and pulled at the knife in his shoulder, Kelly and her co-worker ran past me. Following them into the mall's concourse, I glanced back and saw Ivan and another guard entering the front of the store. The second guard stopped to help his fallen partner, but Ivan leaped over the man and raced after us. Kelly and the young man ran toward a department store. But I had a better idea.

"This way!" I said, waving the two toward the sporting goods store.

I grabbed a metal-framed chair from near a kiosk station on our way to the store, and with both hands and all my might, slammed the chair into the store's glass window. Glass shattered and red and white lights flickered as an alarm blared. Ivan exited the shoe store as the three of us ducked through the broken window and into the sporting goods store. The same leathery, rubbery scent as before struck my nose while we crouch walked through the dark area. We found a small storage closet near the opposite end of the store. While turning to Kelly and her co-worker, I held my index finger to my lips, then pointed at the closet's door. I opened the door and gestured for them to get inside. They quickly complied, and as I eased the door shut, the alarm went silent; the lights stopped flashing, then I heard glass crackle. Two seconds later, more crackling, and a second after that, even more crackles. *All three of them are in here*, I thought as I removed another of my knives. Three of them, three knives. I had a chance, but three of them meant three guns.

Staying close by the wall and in the shadows, I crept in their direction. I heard some whispering that was hard to make out, but there were five words I heard clearly.

"Kill them. Kill them all," Ivan's muffled voice said.

I'd already knew they were playing for keeps but hearing him say that caused something to click inside me. The three men split up. Ivan went down the center, while the guard with the hurt shoulder covered the right, and the other guard walked to the side closest to me. I removed another knife, crouched lower to the floor, and skulked backward. I stopped when I heard the guard's footsteps creep past me. His steps continued until he was fifteen feet away from me. Then they stopped. I was certain he felt me close by, and I knew I needed to strike first. When he took his first stride toward me, I sprang to my feet and hurled a knife at him. The blade penetrated his neck near his collarbone, and he grunted while waving his arms out to his side. I quickly lobbed the other blade, but he fired a couple of rounds before the knife entered the other side of his neck. The guard dropped his gun, then collapsed to the floor.

Hearing Ivan's and the other guard's voices and footsteps, I immediately crouched and tip-toed along the wall in the opposite direction. I threaded around a few racks and shelves before taking cover behind a display of a running mannequin. Peeking around the display, I saw Ivan and the guard looking at their fallen colleague. I continued to the opposite side of the store and ducked behind a register. While there, I removed my last knife and examined it before exhaling. *Two of them, but one knife.*

"White!" Ivan shouted. "Come out and face us like a man."

"You'd like that," I muttered to myself while scanning the countertop for anything I could use as a weapon, and as I did, a thought occurred to me.

Remaining crouched, I circled the register and headed toward the stairs. The silhouettes of Ivan and the guard were moving toward the mannequin I had taken cover behind. I eased up the steps and when I reached the top, I heard the men's footsteps lurking below near the register. I walked past a few clothing racks and a couple of deer heads until I reached the section I was looking for. Inside of a glass case sat several crossbows and next to it on either side were racks of bows and shelves with arrows. Although I felt the crossbow would be the better tool for the job, I would've had to break the glass to get one, so I used my knife to cut the zip-tie holding one of the bows to the rack. It was a standard wooden, red oak bow, nothing fancy, but more than adequate to get the job done. From a shelf, I grabbed three metal-tipped arrows and sized them to the bow before concluding the length of the arrows was a good match for my wingspan.

"Where are you hiding, White?" Ivan said.

I glanced over the railing, down to the first floor, and saw a big problem. Ivan and the guard approached the closet where Kelly and the young worker hid. Ivan gave the guard a gesture indicating there was a door. As the guard approached the door and placed his hand on the knob, I stood, then slung my last knife at the man. The knife passed directly in front of his face before piercing a canoe on the wall next to him. He fell back from the door and landed on his butt.

"There you go," Ivan said while pointing his gun up at me.

I quickly ducked and grabbed the bow and arrows as four thunderous claps stuffed the store and chunks flung from the second-floor railing. Taking cover behind a large, mobile cupboard filled with boots, I heard Ivan's voice yell.

"You're dead!" he said as his footsteps raced toward the stairs.

I lay the arrows in front of me on the floor and peeked around the cupboard. I had a clear line of sight to the stairs. Steadying the bow against the cupboard, I swiftly settled the arrow's nock onto the bow's string. I then placed the arrow's shaft onto the bow's rest, then drew the string back while peering at the stairs through the bow's sight window. Within seconds, Ivan stomped up the stairs and into my sights. He saw me, but I saw him first. The big man paused in his steps. His lips parted. He looked shocked or confused, or not sure of how he felt. I released the arrow, and it whistled through the air before gashing into the big guy's arm. His gun dropped, and he clenched the arrow jutting from his arm as he stumbled backward. I quickly readied another arrow, and just in time as the guard dodged around Ivan on his way up.

Before the guard stepped onto the floor, I released another arrow and it pierced his good shoulder. His eyes and mouth opened wide, and he flopped backward before tumbling down the stairs. As I nocked another arrow, Ivan picked up his pistol and fired at me. Booms roared through the air and bullets buzzed above me while I dropped to the floor. When I heard Ivan's gun click empty, I stepped from behind the cupboard to find him pulling the arrow from his arm and charging at me. Before I could lift the bow, he tackled me across the floor. My back hit a wall and the bow and arrow in my hand dropped to the floor. Ivan cocked his arm back, then launched a punch at my head. I ducked under the attack and kicked him in the crook of his knee. The big guy fell to that knee, then swung his fist at me. I back-stepped and dodged the punch while dancing a safe distance away.

"You're gonna pay for that," he said while catching his breath.

I sunk into a stance with my fist angled in his direction. Ivan growled, then blitzed at me. He attempted to grab me in another tackle, but I slipped out of his path and kicked the side of his knee. His leg buckled while he threw a left cross. I parried the attack and struck him in the face with two quick right jabs. My opponent growled again before launching his heel at me. His kick surprised me, but I blocked it with my shin as he followed up with a wide hook. I raised both of my arms and they collided with Ivan's bulky arm. The force sent me shuffling to my right and into the railing. The moment I found my footing, Ivan clenched my collar and arched my back over the railing. I grasped his wrist and pushed against his arms, while feeling the heat from the big guy's breath as he panted and struggled to force me over.

"You're done," he said between pants.

I continued to push against his arms. "And you talk too much," I said while wrapping my left leg around one of the railing posts and thrusting my right leg into his groin.

The big guy grunted and loosened his grip on me. I swiftly broke his hold, stood straight, and pressed my thumbs into his eyes while holding his head and kneeing him in the gut. As Ivan doubled over, I clenched the back of his neck, then tossed him over my hip and the railing. He hollered and flopped before his back smacked against the bottom floor. I walked to the stairs, and on my way down, I noticed the guard sprawled on the steps with the arrow sticking out of his shoulder. He groaned while opening his eyes and lifting his head. I planted my heel in his face and he nodded to sleep. On the first level, Ivan lay still on the floor with his eyes open and his mouth moving.

I walked over to him and knelt. "I told you if you pointed a gun at me again, you'd be the one going over the ledge."

He said nothing. Just grunted, then glowered at me.

"And the name is Black—Orlando Black," I said before knocking him out with a jab.

I walked to the storage closet. As I opened the door, Kelly and her young co-worker grabbed each other, trembled, and shrieked.

"It's okay," I said. "They're no longer a threat."

I held the door open, and the two exited the closet. I followed behind them to the front of the store. The door unlocked from the inside, and we exited into the mall's main concourse. As we walked toward the shoe store, sirens echoed faintly in the distance.

I stopped at a hall near a toy store. "The cops will be here soon," I said.

Both Kelly and the young man stopped and turned toward me.

"Ask for agent Deidra Harris with the DEA," I continued.

Kelly stepped toward me. "What about you? Aren't you coming?"

I shook my head.

"Why?"

"It's a long story. Remember, ask for Deidra Harris."

"C'mon, Kelly," the young guy said.

Kelly followed behind him, glancing back at me twice before they entered the shoe store. I watched until they disappeared, then made my way up the hall and toward the exit. Outside, sirens wailed and flashing red and blue lights flooded the parking lot. I looked down a few units and saw three squad cars near the shoe store. I kept my eye on the vehicles as I made my way across the parking lot and to my car. As I approached the Viper, I noticed a familiar silhouette standing near it.

"You were gonna leave without saying goodbye?" Deidra said.

"That was the plan," I said as I stepped to her.

She smiled. "How big of a mess you leave inside?" she asked as she leaned against the car.

I leaned next to her and watched the cops enter the mall. "Not too bad. Navarro's general and two of his guards," I said before sighing.

"What about Long's sister?"

"They're okay?"

"They?"

"Yeah, she was working late tonight with a co-worker."

Deidra nodded for a moment before pushing off the car as if she remembered something. "Oh yeah," she said, extending the bag of clothes I left at Ramos' house. "Here."

I grabbed the bag.

"Vargas left this for you."

"Thanks," I said while opening the bag and rummaging through it.

"I better get inside," Deidra said.

Finding only my clothes inside the bag, I smiled, then looked at Deidra. "Yeah, I told her to ask for you," I said, closing the bag.

Deidra and I stared at each other for a moment.

"Thank you, Black. I really mean that."

"And I really mean it," I said while circling the Viper's hood and walking to the driver's side door. "Next time you need help," I continued, looking at her over the roof. "Just ask for it."

Deidra smiled.

"I mean—ask someone. Don't ask me but ask someone."

Deidra giggled. "Goodbye, Black," she said.

"Goodbye, Agent Harris."

She pivoted away and walked across the parking lot toward the crowd of squad cars. I entered the car and brought the engine to life before glancing at the mall and shaking my head. I took in a deep breath, before exhaling and driving off.

Fourteen minutes later, I was on I-10 East, heading toward

Houston. I debated if I should stop for gas. But since the tank was three quarters full, and I was full of adrenaline, I figured I'd take my chances with a gas station closer to Houston. Figured I'd find a hotel and sleep for twelve hours straight. Figured afterwards I'd continue heading east, or maybe north. Smiling, I scoffed at the thought, then shrugged at the wheel.

Who knows?

THANK YOU FOR READING

I have a favor to ask. If you have a moment, I would really appreciate it if you could leave a short review on the page where you purchased this book. I'm thankful for you sharing your feedback about this book. It really helps new readers find this series.

Sign up for notifications of new books by Alex Cage and exclusive giveaways

www.AlexCage.com/signup

ALSO BY ALEX CAGE

More books by Alex Cage. Have you read them all? Grab your next adventure today!

Orlando Black Series

Carolina Dance

Bayside Boom

Family Famous (Novella)

Bet on Black

Leroy Silver Series

Contracts & Bullets

Aloha & Bullets

Get the latest releases and exclusive giveaways, sign up to the Alex Cage Reader List.

www.AlexCage.com/signup

JOIN THE READER'S LIST

Get the latest releases and exclusive giveaways - sign up to the Alex Cage Reader List:

www.AlexCage.com/signup

ABOUT THE AUTHOR

Alex Cage is a thriller author and passionate wordsmith who loves to blend his fascination with martial arts and travel with high-octane action and explosive adventures. He enjoys nothing more than entertaining his readers with death-defying missions, larger-than-life characters, and suspenseful stories that always find a way to keep you on your toes.

As the author of nearly a dozen titles, including the Orlando Black series and the Leroy Silver series, Alex combines his obsession for thrillers with a sprinkling of fantasy and sci-fi, so that readers will always find something to capture their imagination. He currently resides in North Carolina. When not writing his next novel, you can find him reading and practicing martial arts.

Find out more about Alex Cage (and get a free read):

www.alexcage.com
connect@alexcage.com

CLEAN FAST-PACED ACTION THRILLERS

Made in the USA
Monee, IL
11 July 2023

38979474R00132